Treaty Brides

THE
DIPLOMAT'S
BRIDE

SAMANTHA CAYTO

The Diplomat's Bride
ISBN # 978-1-80250-959-5
©Copyright Samantha Cayto 2022
Cover Art by Fiona Jayde ©Copyright June 2022
Interior text design by Claire Siemaszkiewicz
Pride Publishing

Published in 2022 by Pride Publishing, United Kingdom.

Pride Publishing is an imprint of Totally Entwined Group Limited.

THE
DIPLOMAT'S
BRIDE

Chapter One

Benedict, Lord Tentrees of Northcliff, stood at the balcony's rail and peered down at the colorful spectacle of the servants' ball. Technically, he had no business being there. The ball season for the nobility had already ended earlier in the evening. These final hours were intended to benefit those who served the palace denizens so faithfully throughout the year. This was a grand gesture of thanks for their hard work and loyalty. Woe be it to anyone who didn't give a servant these few hours to enjoy themselves with food, drink and merriment. The royal family had long made it clear that this was by decree. There would be some aching heads and sleepy eyes come the harsh light of the morning, but for now, the people twirling around the dance floor and taking liberties with each other in corners had no care in the world—or so it seemed to him. Not that his gaze landed on anyone for long, because he was there to find one person in particular.

It wasn't difficult for him to spot his quarry. Even among the bright garments of the attendants, Kexen of the Outer Vale stood out. He was clothed in the colors of fall—deep red, bright orange and sparkling yellow. His daringly short doublet sported gathered sleeves that cascaded in folds down his slender arms while provocatively highlighting what lay behind the crotch of his almost obscenely snug trousers. His knee-high brown leather boots gave his legs an even longer look, while his elaborately braided hair swung with his every graceful turn. Kexen was not a tall man, but that was all to the good. The boy would fit perfectly with Ben's own height. The vision of gathering him in his arms was captivating. His cock hardened at the thought of it, enjoying the spark of pleasure. With his demanding profession, there wasn't much opportunity to slake his needs. Hopefully, that situation was about to change.

There was no reason to tarry any longer, so, stepping away from his vantage point, he headed toward the staircase that would send him into the midst of the revelers. He had intended to be as inconspicuous as possible, understanding that this was not his domain, that he was an interloper who might cause some alarm among the servants. His good intentions notwithstanding, the severity of his all-black clothing served to make him stand out among the festive outfits of those around him. There was a certain amount of startlement by those who saw and recognized his station, if not his identity, leading to smiles morphing into more respectful expressions. Some nodding of heads occurred, as well, in deference to his rank. Ben tried to convey that he was no threat to them, that he had no demands, not even any expectations—not from these people, in any event. Kexen was a different story altogether. If all went to plan, Ben would seduce the boy while judging up close whether they would make a good match.

Ben caught sight of Kexen on the dance floor again. He was being whirled around in the beefy arms of a footman. Ben settled against the wall to stay unobtrusive as he waited with less patience than he would have expected from himself for the musicians to end their song. The moment the last of the notes were played, he launched into the crowd. Now he appreciated being shown respect as the partying servants cleared a way for him, making his journey that much quicker. He caught up with Kexen and his partner just as they were stepping out onto one of the balconies. The night was brisk but, in contrast to the heat of the ballroom, very refreshing—not that the cold air served to dampen his ardor. Seeing Kexen up close only increased his desire for the boy.

Exquisite.

Kexen's face was lit with joviality as he gazed up at the footman, laughing at something the man had said. There was a coy look to the boy's expression, as well. Ben was surprised at the spurt of jealousy he felt at the sight. He reminded himself that Kexen was not his and might never be so unless he proved to be worthy. Charging forth as if he were an enraged lover was hardly going to serve that purpose. Being a diplomat, he knew how to bank his emotions and measure his words and actions. By the time he reached the couple, he hoped he appeared friendly and casual.

Kexen was the first to spot him. His jubilance dimmed somewhat, although he looked more curious than apprehensive. He nodded his head. "My lord, is there something you wish?"

You. In my bed. Ben didn't voice this desire out loud, of course. Instead, he said, "I would love a dance, if you would honor me." Ben had the pleasure of seeing surprise flash across the boy's face. He was delighted that the obviously confident young man could still be caught off guard.

Kexen reached to twist one finger around the chain of a small ruby pendant and dropped his gaze. "I am honored, my lord. But your pardon, this is the servants' ball. It is not fit for a nobleman." Just as Ben was appreciating the subtlety of the rebuke, Kexen looked up at him from under his lashes.

Cheeky boy, you're interested. Ben stepped closer. "And a fine event it is. Please forgive the intrusion, but I have been anticipating the opportunity to meet you, Kexen of the Outer Vale. This seemed the best occasion to do so."

Now Kexen showed open welcome, his lips curling in a beckoning smile. "Oh. You flatter me, my lord."

The footman proved that his brains weren't as big as his muscles. When the man opened his mouth as if to object, Ben stepped deftly between him and Kexen and stared the footman down. "If you don't mind?"

They were matched in height, and while Ben wasn't quite as broad, he could hold his own in a brawl as well as at the negotiation table—not that either skill was required in this event. He didn't hesitate to convey his social position in his gaze to encourage the footman to find someone else to dally with. The man was confident but not entirely stupid, apparently. With a curt nod, he strode away.

Pleased with the outcome, Ben turned to Kexen and held out his hand. "They are playing a waltz…my favorite."

Kexen managed to convey shyness, something his reputation belied. Ben didn't mind the pretext. The boy's ability to navigate the complex waters of a court was one of the things that Ben coveted him for. He hadn't been worried about a refusal, but when Kexen put his hand in his own, the jolt of excitement Ben felt was a surprise. He prided himself on being cool and measured in his actions. Something about the feel of this boy, however, made him want to drag him off into a corner and do a different kind of dance — one that involved his cock sliding past those slightly tinted and lovely lips. The way Kexen closed the distance between them, wrapping his arm around Ben's neck, told him that the boy had similar ideas. Such a temptation, but Ben schooled himself to be patient, because this night was not a one-time seduction. It was hopefully the beginning of a short courtship.

Ben took his dance partner by the waist and pulled him in close, letting Kexen feel the measure of his arousal. "Let us stay out here. I wouldn't want my presence to impede the others' enjoyment. I will endeavor to keep you warm." So saying, he began to slowly lead the boy in circles.

Kexen tilted his head to look him in the eye. "You are succeeding admirably, my lord."

"I'm gratified to hear it. I'm Benedict, by the way."

"I know who you are, Lord Tentrees. I must confess to being surprised that you know who I am."

Ben whirled them into the far recesses of the balcony, taking them away from everyone else. "You shouldn't be. Who at the palace hasn't heard of the valiant groomer of the Duchess of Vostguard? You helped to save Prince Soren from an ambush at grave risk to your own safety."

Kexen dropped his gaze and shrugged. "Oh, that. It was all the Duchess' doing. I merely went along to serve him, as is my duty."

Ben knew false modesty when he heard it, and this was decidedly *not* that. Kexen truly believed his actions weren't worthy of special mention. Ben's estimation of him increased. There was more to this boy than beauty and even bravery. Most people in his position would brag to anyone and everyone about such exploits, not caring if their words betrayed the secrets of those whom they served. Kexen's humbleness and discretion were excellent traits in diplomatic circles. There was no doubt in Ben's mind that he had made the right choice, even if it were really the only one afforded him.

"You don't do yourself justice. I've attended a few meetings in the presence of the king. I assure you he feels quite differently."

Kexen blushed despite the cold air swirling around them. "The royal family is very kind, my lord."

"My friends call me Ben."

"I am surely not that upon such a short acquaintance."

"I should like you to be." He let his passion show in his eyes. "Should we continue our dance somewhere more private inside?" He actually held his breath waiting for the reply. In theory, he could have his way whether Kexen wanted him or not. King Auden didn't tolerate the abuse of servants, but pressure could be brought to bear quietly against even the most secure servants with little retribution, if one was careful about it. But that wasn't how he intended this venture to go. An eager Kexen would be a far better prize than a reluctant and begrudging one.

Kexen rested his cheek on Ben's shoulder. "I would like that very much."

Ben wasted no time, ending their dance before tugging Kexen by the hand back into the ballroom. He skirted the crowd to leave through the nearest exit and led the boy to the first quiet alcove he could find. The palace had so many discreet places for assignations that he was inclined to believe it was by deliberate design. Part of him disliked being so public. He would have preferred to take Kexen back to his own apartment, but, despite his recent promotion in the diplomatic corps, he still didn't have a room in the palace. Taking the time to dress for outside and head to his place in the city didn't appeal to him. Plus, he didn't want to burden Kexen with two trips—there and back—on such a cold and late night.

The moment they were out of the sight of prying eyes, he pulled the boy into a kiss. He'd intended to take it slowly, to do nothing that might alarm even an experienced person such as Kexen. One touch of their lips, however, had him devouring the boy's mouth instead. His much-valued control snapped with a speed that alarmed him. Or, rather, it would have, if feasting on Kexen were not as delectable as it was. Within seconds, he was sitting on a tufted settee with Kexen straddling his lap. Their respective erections mashed against each other as much as their clothing allowed. Ben wanted nothing more than to strip those barriers away. He had to wrestle with himself to gain control over his passion.

Breaking the kiss, he peppered Kexen's jaw with quick pecks. "We must slow down, my dear, or I won't last much longer."

Kexen giggled in a sweet voice. "Who says I want you to...*Ben*?"

Hearing his name spoken in a voice thick with need nearly sent him over the edge. He closed his eyes and nuzzled the side of the boy's neck, breathing in the sharp scent of bergamot mixed with the more musky smell of his arousal. As Ben worried that his mind was becoming cloudy, Kexen slipped from his grasp and was kneeling between his legs before Ben knew what was happening.

"Let me make you happy." That was all the boy said before undoing the laces of Ben's trousers, freeing his cock.

What rational thought that was left in his mind fled in the next instance when Kexen swallowed him whole right down nearly to the root. It was an impressive feat based on his prior experience. No one had ever taken the entirety of his rather large dick, and few had been able to manage as much as Kexen was now. The intensity of being mostly encased in such tight, wet heat nearly undid him. Then Kexen worked his throat muscles to massage the top half of Ben's shaft. That was all it took for him to double over from his orgasm, pressing his lips tight to keep from shouting his pleasure.

Kexen kept lavishing attention on Ben's dick until it popped out of his mouth. The boy beamed up at him as Ben caught his breath. "Do you feel better now, my lord?"

By way of an answer, Ben hauled him back up to his lap with a swiftness that made Kexen gasp. "Not nearly enough. I want more." He kissed the boy again, tasting his own bitterness. Far from being disgusted, he loved it, because it was a mingling of them both. He wanted to reciprocate the giving of such pleasure. But when he reached between them to cup Kexen's erection, he found that the boy had already come from the cocksucking alone. Knowing that he'd had such a potent effect on him puffed up his chest. He wondered if he could do it again and found himself eager to try. There was plenty of time left in the night, and based on the way Kexen melted into his arms, he seemed just as eager for more.

This was proof that he'd been right all along. Kexen of the Outer Vale was the perfect bride for him.

* * * *

"Ow!" The Duchess of Vostguard put his hand to his head as he frowned at Kexen through his reflection in the mirror. "What has my hair done to offend you this morning?"

Mortified, Kexen hurried to make amends. "I beg your pardon, Your Grace. I'm all sixes and sevens today."

"So I have observed." The duchess grinned. "I suppose the servants' ball went to the wee hours. I'm not surprised you're tired. Thank the gods the season is over. I don't think I could stand another night of feasting and dancing. Such a waste," he added with a shake of his head. Being a Marsher by birth, the man was still not used to the excesses of the Moorcondian palace.

Kexen resumed brushing his head, more careful in dealing with the snarls. He'd been woolgathering, reliving the exquisite and all-too-short time he'd shared with Lord Tentrees and hoping it hadn't been a gentle form of dismissal when the man had sent him off to bed with promises of them seeing each other again. The mere thought of kissing the nobleman and more sent Kexen's body into a state of painful arousal. He'd been careful to wear loose trousers and a long tunic, both to ease his aching cock and to hide his undiminished happiness. The duchess didn't need a hard shaft poking the back of his head.

Kexen made idle chit-chat to take his mind off the previous night's pleasures. "All will be relatively quiet for a while now until the snow comes. Then it will be time for the winter festival. It goes on in various ways until spring. There's so much fun to be had." Satisfied with the silky fall of his duchess's hair, he began to plait it in the simple style his master preferred.

The duchess grinned. "I am looking forward to that, actually. Occasionally we get a light frost in the Marshlands, but I've never truly experienced snow."

Kexen smiled at the man's reflection. "I think you will love the sporting events, and there are sleigh rides and ice skating, hot chocolate by the barrelful and flavored treats made out of shaved ice. I'm sure the prince is looking forward to introducing you to all of it."

"I expect you're right. Soren says he loves experiencing everything through my eyes. It makes it fresh for him."

Kexen scrutinized his work and, satisfied, stood back to let the duchess rise to be dressed. "You and the prince can still ride, too. Moorcondian steeds are used to prancing through the snow."

"So I've heard. It's sounds very exciting." The duchess stood still as Kexen removed his robe and began to dress him for the day. While it was obvious to him that the duchess was still not comfortable with being pampered in such a way, they'd developed a good rhythm in handling it. "That reminds me, Kexen. The prince has had a delivery of horses for you to choose from."

This news was not unexpected, and while he was excited at the prospect of gaining a new mount, he was also becoming embarrassed at the gifts being showered on him by the royal couple. "Oh, Your Grace, you'll spoil me. It's truly not necessary." Kexen turned the man so that he could see his reflection in the long mirror. The duchess's mode of dress was quite simple, being a long kirtle with matching trousers. There would be less fun to be had in choosing his outfits now that the ball season was over, although they'd barely started planning out the winter wardrobe. That was something exciting to look forward to.

The duchess turned this way and that before saying, "We're going to have to disagree on that point, Kexen. There aren't enough gifts in the world for me to show how much I value what you've done for me and my husband. Soren feels the same way." He turned to grin at him directly. "You're just going to have to get used to being spoiled."

Kexen returned the look and sighed dramatically. "I suppose I'll manage." When the duchess stood scrutinizing him, he asked, "What is it, Your Grace?"

"I don't know exactly. You seem particularly... *satisfied* this morning. And your mind has been elsewhere. I suppose you dallied with an especially appealing man at the ball?"

Kexen's cheeks heated with embarrassment. It wasn't like him to be so when the issue of men arose. And because he'd developed something of a friendship with the duchess and trusted him entirely, he readily confessed that it was true. "I did, as it happens. A nobleman," he added in a low voice as if it were a great secret.

The duchess raised his eyebrows. "What was a nobleman doing at the servants' ball?"

"Looking for me, or so he said." The fact that such a dashing man as Benedict had sought him out especially was astounding to him and made him want to preen with pride.

"Who was it?"

"Lord Tentrees...the diplomat," he added.

The duchess pursed his lips. "I know of him. We've been introduced, at least, and I believe I've heard that he's doing quite well in service to the king. He's very handsome, too, is he not?"

Kexen grinned broadly. "Yes, he is. And he's not some soft nobleman. I could feel the strength of his muscles as I held on to him." He didn't add that the man had been blessed with a long, thick cock. The duchess wasn't comfortable with such frank talk.

"Hmm-m. I suppose there's no harm in it, so long as you had a good time. Be careful, though. I don't like the idea of these noblemen taking advantage of you, Kexen."

"Be at ease about that, Your Grace. Lord Tentrees was every bit a gentleman, and I probably won't even see him again." That last thought made him sad. Funny, that. He wasn't one to pine after any one man. There was something different about Benedict, however. *Ben.* He had said they were friends. Kexen could only hope that would prove to be true.

Chapter Two

"Sir Rolf!" Ben hurried to catch up with Prince Soren's liege man before he disappeared around the hall corner.

The Outer Vale man stopped and turned with obvious annoyance until he saw who called him. He plastered a respectful look on his face and nodded his head once Ben stopped in front of him. "Lord Tentrees."

"I would like a word, if you have the time." Oddly, Ben felt somewhat nervous. That wasn't like him. He was known for remaining cool under pressure. This talk with Kexen's relative shouldn't inspire any concern. The outcome of it was obvious. *I hope.*

"Certainly, my lord. How may I be of service?"

Ben stood with legs braced and hands clasped behind his back. He reminded himself this was simply a negotiation. "You are the guardian of your cousin, Kexen, are you not?"

The soldier stiffened noticeably. "I am. Is there a problem, my lord?"

Ben tried to be disarming with a smile and gentle tone. "Certainly not. Quite the contrary, in fact." He took in a deep breath and let it out slowly and silently. This was a trick he'd learned from his mentor at the university, and it had served him well so far. "I am asking for his hand in marriage." At the man's obviously perplexed look, Ben hurried to explain. "I am soon to go on a diplomatic mission that will last the entire winter. I am in need of a wife, and as women do not interest me overly much and with the precedent set by Prince Soren, I have decided to find my own male bride."

"Kexen?" Now the man conveyed how skeptical he was of this pronouncement. "He's a boy of the merchant class."

"I am aware, and that's one of the reasons he makes a perfect choice. Please let me explain. I hail from Northcliff, as you may be aware. My family keeps a large apiary and has done so for generations. Our honey is second to none. Your family," he continued on surer footing now that he was getting into the practical details, "is well known for its mead."

"No one makes it better. We supply the palace with it for the royal family." There was pride in the man's eyes, an encouraging sign.

"I am also aware, and I bet it's quite lucrative, as it should be — but not as much as it could be probably, as I imagine you pay dearly for your large honey supply." When Rolf nodded in agreement, Ben got to the heart of his offer. "If you agree on your family's behalf to give Kexen to me as my bride, I have the authority to bind a trading deal between our families. You will have a steady supply of the best honey at a favorable price, my family will have a reliable source to sell it and I get a fetching bride to take with me on my diplomatic missions."

"An intriguing offer, my lord, and one that I could agree to on behalf of my family and its interests. There is one obvious impediment, however. Kexen is not a commodity. Our family will not force him into marriage for the sake of a trade agreement, no matter how lucrative. And he's barely eighteen, young to wed."

Ben had anticipated this response and that was why he'd approached Kexen first for a bit of seduction. He wanted a willing wife, not one dragged into it by his family. Given the boy's reputation around the palace, Ben had also to assume Sir Rolf knew him to be anything but an innocent, making the issue of maturity a moot one. "Old enough. He has been quite free in his actions in the palace, as I understand it," Ben said with as much delicacy as he could. "You don't keep him tethered close."

Sir Rolf's face betrayed a hint of umbrage before he quickly masked it. "Of course not. He's a bright boy, and like any of his age, in need of experiencing life for himself. Telling Kexen what to do has also never been very effective," he added almost to himself. "That doesn't change the fact that my guardianship is a loose one at best, and to the extent I have power over him, I would never force him into marriage."

"Nor would I want you to," Ben was quick to reassure the man. "He and I have met recently, and he seemed rather open to my...overture. I think we'd make an excellent match, and there is some time for us to get to know each other before I must leave for the Iron Shore."

Now Rolf looked pensive. "An important treaty mission, to be sure."

"Indeed. We cannot let Far Isle gain an exclusive trading agreement for the iron ore. The new queen is said to be both flighty and strong-headed. She has determined that only one treaty shall be signed and has set the winter months for us and Far Isle to dance attendance on her and convince her who is more deserving. Having a strong wife who is well-versed in the workings of a court will be very important to my success." This was only part of the reason he sought to marry the Outer Vale boy, but he intended to reserve the rest of his mission planning for his future bride's ears alone.

"Well, Kexen is suited for the role, I have to admit. And the trade agreement would be most welcome. He is, at the end of the day, devoted to his family. If he wants you, I will agree to it, but only if he convinces me that his decision is motivated by more than duty."

This was not quite the definitive answer Ben had been hoping for. Still, it was a step in the right direction, and he was confident he could win over Kexen. "That is more than fair, Sir Rolf. I have the proposed trade agreement already drafted and ready for your review, any time you are free to do so."

Sir Rolf banked his expression. "I will pay you a visit right before the evening meal, if that suits."

"Certainly. But might I suggest we meet in the blue card room? My apartment is in the city and not convenient for such matters."

"As you wish. And, my lord, I would ask that you not approach Kexen again until I've done so. *If* he is to be your wife, I insist that decorum be observed until the ceremony that will bind you to each other. Our family is flexible in its thinking but also very protective of its members. I will not have the boy deciding something so momentous using any organ other than his brain and possibly his heart. I trust I've made my point."

Prince Soren's liege man was nothing if not courageous. He was bold to put the honor and personal interests of his cousin above what might be politically safer. And he was clearly not intimidated by Ben's lofty standing. The man would make a great ally and a formidable foe. Ben intended to make him the former. "Of course. I would have it no other way." He had no trouble being sincere, as it was the truth. Now that he was determined to make Kexen his bride, there would be no more assignations in alcoves. Their wedding night would come soon enough.

"And I realize I've left out the most important point for your consideration. I will be good to him, Sir Rolf. Your cousin will want for nothing, and I will treat him tenderly. You have my word on this."

"Thank you for the reassurance, my lord. My family and I would expect nothing less. Until this evening…" With a quick nod of his head, Sir Rolf left.

Ben took a moment to bask in the success of this first meeting before leaving the palace. The cold had already settled in for the season, and being so high up, the city was bathed in brisk wind. He pulled his cloak tighter around him as he made his way to his nearby apartment. Being an optimistic man, he intended to operate on the assumption that the trade agreement would go through and he'd be bringing his new bride to the Iron Shore. That required some planning, as the new Lady Tentrees would need a maid. It didn't matter that the boy currently served in that capacity for the Duchess of Vostguard. His new station in life would dictate being catered to. Ben could only hope that his plans in this regard would be well-received.

His journey was short, as he could afford rooms close to the palace. The accommodations were fine for a bachelor but cramped for a family. When they returned from the Iron Shore mission — triumphant — he would leverage the success into hopefully a suite in the palace. It would advance his career to be so close to the seat of power, and his bride would almost certainly appreciate living there, as well. It caught him short for a moment as he considered how much he wanted to please Kexen and give him a wonderful life, filled with excitement and as much luxury as he could manage. The vows he'd given Sir Rolf were not mere words to be persuasive. He'd meant every one of them, determined to be a good husband.

When he entered his sitting room, he found two people standing ramrod like soldiers. One was known to him. Baldrick had been his valet ever since his university days. The older man was meticulous and a stickler for both propriety and detail. His value to Ben now that he was a diplomat was incalculable. There was no one he trusted more. The woman beside Baldrick was a stranger to Ben, but, given that she was a close copy of Baldrick, he had to assume this was the man's sister, Euphemia. She was almost the same height as her brother, somewhat broader and sporting a short haircut that was daringly out of fashion for anyone, let alone a woman.

"Welcome home, my lord," Baldrick intoned. "I trust your venture went well."

"Indeed." Ben whipped off his cloak and tossed it over the back of a chair as he went to warm his hands by the fire Baldrick had laid that morning. "I believe there shall be a Lady Tentrees as early as the week's end."

Baldrick went to pick up the cloak. "Excellent news, my lord. My sister's arrival is timely."

"You did say to make haste, brother," the woman said, remaining rooted to her spot.

Ben turned his back to the fireplace and studied her. He couldn't help but second-guess his idea of having an older woman act as lady's maid to his bride. Perhaps a younger one would have made him more comfortable, given that finding another 'Kexen' to serve the purpose was both unlikely and unwise, because of their somewhat conservative destination. "And you have experience in such service as I require?"

Euphemia gave him a direct look—not insolent, but confident. "I do, my lord. I have dressed ladies since I was thirteen, even though I have little interest in such matters myself."

"I see." Being a lady's maid seemed an odd choice for her to make based on that statement, although perhaps she'd had few choices. "And you understand that my bride will be somewhat unconventional?"

"If by that you mean that you're marrying another man, my lord, then yes. As long as he doesn't mind wearing dresses, I dare say I will prove useful to him. And I'll take no mind of his form," she added with a quick smile that Ben found surprisingly disarming. "The male body holds no interest for me."

"Excellent. And as I will be providing the trousseau, I want you to be as helpful as my bride will permit. No expense will be spared."

Ben spoke with more certainty than he felt. The deal was yet to be made, and there was no assurance that it would be. Sir Rolf had been more tentative than he'd expected, and there was the matter of whether the boy would accept the match. *He* has *to.* The vehemence of his thought surprised him. The diplomatic mission be damned. Now that he'd held the boy in his arms, had experienced the delight of his luscious lips wrapped around his cock, Ben found he looked forward to the marriage. And it wasn't merely a desire to be wed to a pretty and biddable lad. He wanted this boy. He wanted *Kexen.*

* * * *

"It makes no sense to leave this as your bedroom, Soren. You spend every night with me, so what's the point of taking up space for things you never use anymore?"

"I can't argue with your logic, my dear."

The prince stood next to his wife, staring at the large, ornately carved bed that was clean and fresh, if for no other reason than the one the duchess had given. It was never used. Like any gentleman, the prince went to his wife for conjugal relations — and never the reverse. There was nothing unusual in the use of the duchess's bed. It was the *frequency* that caused this room the three of them stood in to be pointless. Kexen was pretty sure most married couples didn't dally every night with each other. And even among those who did, what made this royal couple different was that the prince stayed with his wife the whole night. It was, in Kexen's eyes, the most obvious proof that this was a love match. The romantic in him applauded it all, but it meant that this room wasn't used for any purpose other than to dress. It was no surprise that the practical part of the duchess saw it as a waste.

"What would you have me do about it?" the prince continued.

"Turn it into a private sitting room, somewhere that you can relax or work, at your discretion, but with no one needing to be entertained. Your receiving room can become more of an office, big enough to receive members of the court for official business without having to remove anything personal that you don't want to share with others."

The duchess moved closer to the doorway between the two rooms being discussed and spread his arms wide. "This will become a clear line between the prince and the man that you can use any time of the day. It will become your haven." The duchess beamed at his husband.

"A fine idea, I have to admit. But you will join me in my private domain, will you not?" The prince sent a heated look to his wife that Kexen didn't miss, even from where he stood awkwardly waiting for the duchess to call on his service. As always, he envied the passion between them.

The duchess's cheeks pinked, and he lowered his gaze. "If you ask me to."

Just when Kexen began to feel as if the prince's bed was going to get a fervid sendoff, voices could be heard coming from the prince's receiving room, his cousin's being one of them. Kexen thought nothing of it, given how close Rolf was to the prince. It was likewise commonplace when Deward appeared in the doorway to request his master's presence. After the trusted servant shut the door, Kexen knew there must be some important business of the realm to deal with. He hoped it had nothing to do with the Marshers or anyone else that would lead to yet another war. The duchess shot him a worried look, and Kexen did his best to convey confidence that this was no more than the usual workings of the place until Deward begged the duchess's pardon and asked him — and only him — to join the prince that alarm bells started ringing.

Don't be such a ninny. This has nothing to do with you. It's none of your business, that's all.

His own reassurance lasted only a few minutes, because the duchess himself came to the door next and bid Kexen to join them. There was a look of worry in the man's eyes that he couldn't quite bank. Kexen tried to remain calm. As he entered the room, however, the expressions on both the prince's face and Rolf's broke his reserve. "Is someone dead?" Visions of his parents, siblings and other family members raced through his head as he steeled himself for the worst.

The duchess was the first to answer. "No!" He took Kexen's hand. "I'm sorry for the drama. It's just that Rolf has some news — good news, I think," he added with a slight grimace, belaying his words.

Kexen looked at his cousin. "What is it?"

Appearing surprisingly uncomfortable, Rolf took a step toward him. "I've been approached by a gentleman who desires to make you his wife."

It took a few seconds for the meaning to sink in. Once it did, Kexen couldn't stifle a chuckle. "Really? How absurd." Remembering in whose presence he stood, he hastily clarified. "I mean that it's ridiculous that anyone would want to marry me. Who is it?" As he waited for the answer, he sifted through his memories to see if he'd somehow led one of his admirers to think there was more to their relationship than a bit of fun.

"Benedict…Lord Tentrees."

The answer floored him. If not for the duchess still holding his hand, he might have toppled over. "That's ludicrous," he blurted out, the first words he could think of. "This has to be a joke."

Rolf shook his head. "I assure you, it's not. He has presented a trade agreement between our families, whereby we can source their excellent honey on an exclusive and discounted basis so long as you bind the contract with your body. It is a very fine arrangement," Rolf added with some obvious reluctance.

"Oh." He must have swayed because the next thing he knew, the duchess had steered him to a chair and sat him down. The impudence of sitting while his masters stood in front of him would have appalled him if his mind weren't reeling from the news.

Kexen looked at Rolf again. "I'm not sure I truly understand. I barely know Lord Tentrees."

Rolf's lips formed a straight line before he answered. "Apparently you made a favorable *impression* on the man the night of the servants' ball."

Kexen felt his cheeks warm. He was never prone to embarrassment, but somehow the mention of that brief encounter turned him shy in front of these other men. "It was a small dalliance, nothing of note." Despite his own words, his mind conjured up the very pleasant memories of the night and how attracted to the young lord he'd been...and remained. "Surely he only wants me as an exclusive lover?" He'd almost said 'mistress', as that word fit better. Powerful men often took lower class women as playthings by bribing the family. It was a considerable step up from the outright capturing and rape of long ago, yet no one could claim that it was truly consensual, given the pressure on those women to accede.

Rolf pressed a palm against his forehead. "No. I'm doing a poor job of this if I've left you in any doubt about the arrangement. He wants to marry you, Kexen, in the legally binding sense."

"Oh." Despite his training, he settled back into the cushions of the chair, unable to rise given the sudden weakening of his knees.

Kexen hadn't seen this coming at all. Despite the precedent set by the royal couple in the room, a marriage between two men was still unheard of. He'd assumed marriage was not for him, given that he had put his lack of interest in women to the test early upon his arrival at the palace. The results of that encounter had been definitive. He desired men exclusively, but this offer from one had blindsided him. It was hard to imagine how it would benefit him personally. Being a wife was a more secure position than a lover, but it still meant giving up his freedom and being under the control of another. Because he was of the noble class, Lord Tentrees would always be the master of their marriage. Kexen wasn't sure he liked that idea.

"I would become Lady Tentrees?" He glanced at the duchess, whose hand remained clasped with his, a steady show of support that Kexen appreciated. It also gave him his answer, of course. Having no title of his own, his husband's would define him legally.

"I hadn't really thought about it," Rolf confessed. "I suppose so." He looked at the prince.

"Indeed. And as the diplomat's bride, you will be expected to travel with him for all his missions. Wives are considered an important part of the job, facilitating the social requirements and forging ties with foreigners that might prove useful in the future. Only pregnancy puts an end to that—which, of course, won't be a problem in this case," he added, rubbing at one earlobe with a thoughtful look on his face. Even the prince was struggling to absorb the news, apparently.

Kexen latched onto that point. "Oh, but surely that's an impediment for Lord Tentrees. I can't give him an heir."

"I raised that point as I reviewed the offered agreement," Rolf said. "As a younger son, he has no familial expectations in that regard. And he says it's of no importance to him personally. He likes men in general...and you in particular. That's all that matters to him."

"I see." Kexen went silent for a while as he contemplated his fate. When he'd thought about his future, he'd pictured eventually finding his one true love and settling into a permanent relationship. But that had always been something he'd pictured for later in his life, after he'd enjoyed what youth and living in the palace brought him. He took great pleasure in experiencing a variety of other men and wasn't ready to tie himself to one man so soon. And he'd never expected to marry anyone, let alone a nobleman such as Lord Tentrees. He could do worse, he supposed. The man was devastatingly handsome, the epitome of masculinity and just the sort of man Kexen had always been attracted to. He was charming, as well, which hopefully meant that he had a pleasant demeanor in general. Being married to a surly or even abusive man wasn't something he could imagine tolerating.

There were more important issues at play, however, than Kexen's personal happiness. "It is a good agreement for the family, you say?"

"Very," Rolf confirmed. "That being said, you know we will not sacrifice you for the sake of a trade deal. If you don't want this man, then that is that."

Kexen peered at the concerned faces surrounding him, marveling that people as important as the prince and the duchess would worry themselves over his future. "I do like him."

The duchess squeezed his hand. "You hardly know him. This would be forever, Kexen. You must not make a hasty decision."

While he appreciated the advice, he also knew what lay unspoken was how the Marsher boy had been given *no* choice in his husband. The duchess clearly didn't want the same fate for Kexen, yet the royal marriage had proven to be the perfect match. Love could come from so little. There was no reason why he wouldn't fall in love with Ben. If nothing else, he expected sex would be most satisfying, and if that was all they had between them, so be it. Regardless of what everyone was saying, Kexen understood his duty to his family and his country. And he did relish the excitement that came from living within a royal court. He'd make an excellent diplomat's bride — of that, he was sure.

He took a deep breath for courage before he could change his mind. "I accept. Please tell Lord Tentrees that I will become his wife."

Rolf studied him shrewdly for a few seconds before saying, "Very well. I can find nothing objectionable about him, based on my inquiries."

"He does have a good reputation," the prince confirmed. "I have heard nothing that blemishes his character, and he has the king's confidence in his diplomatic skills. His reputation is one of confident drive bolstered by equanimity. How he might act in private is another matter, of course. A man can have two faces and be good at hiding the one he doesn't want others to see. Regardless, I have no reason to question Lord Tentrees' temperament."

The prince's words weren't all that reassuring. Still, Kexen said, "Thank you, Your Highness. I appreciate your opinion."

Rolf chimed in with better news. "And I added in a clause to the agreement that you must be permitted to visit your family at least twice a year, his duties permitting. Plus, they pay a steep penalty if Tentrees treats you badly." Rolf leaned toward him with a stern look. "You must swear to tell me if he does."

Touched, Kexen reassured his cousin, "I promise I will." Even as he said the words, however, he wasn't sure he meant them. Once married, he would be emancipated from his family, if not his husband. He needed to stand on his own feet and deal with whatever trouble his marriage brought. A picture of Ben smiling at him made it impossible for him to imagine the man ever hurting him, so the promise was an easy one.

The duchess took everyone's attention. "Soren, now would be an excellent time to give Kexen our gift."

"I agree." The prince strode over to his desk.

Kexen looked up at his master. "Your Grace? You have given me so much, surely I am deserving of nothing more."

The duchess dismissed that statement. "Let us be the judge of that. We've showered you with mere fripperies. Your service has gone above and beyond and calls for a larger measure of our gratitude."

A thought suddenly occurred to Kexen as the reality of his circumstances started to sink in. "Oh, Your Grace, who will dress you if I am wed and gone from the palace?" He loved his job and had assumed to keep it for many years, if not for the rest of his life.

"Don't worry about that. We'll find someone suitable to replace you. Having done the hard work of creating the right style for me, I'm sure someone clever will follow it. I shall miss you, however," the man added with a wan smile. "And when you return, we can be friends for once…and not master and servant."

Kexen didn't have time to contemplate that happy future because the prince returned and held out a thick piece of paper tied with a dark blue ribbon and sporting the prince's seal. Kexen had to release the duchess's hand to take it. He stared at the weighty document, not able to imagine what it was until Rolf cleared his throat and nodded at it. Understanding, Kexen broke the seal and unfolded the paper. He stared at the words but he didn't truly fathom their import. He shook his head. "Your Highness?"

"That is a deed, Kexen, for a free-holding on the border of Vostguard and the Outer Vale. It contains a small cottage with fifteen rooms, a stable and thirty tenant farmers. It generates a fine annual income. The previous owner died last summer with no heirs. It reverted to me, and I've been waiting for the right person to bestow it on. That would be you." The prince grinned broadly, holding out his hand until his duchess went into his embrace. Then they both smiled at him.

Kexen's fingers went lax, causing him to almost drop the precious document. "I-I don't know what to say."

"Good gods, boy," Rolf said, "say 'thank you'."

Kexen jumped to his feet. "Oh yes, of course. Thank you, Your Highness, Your Grace. This a most marvelous gift. Too good for the likes of me, especially now that I'm going to be married. Surely Ben must stay by the palace when he's not on a mission. We won't be able to enjoy this."

The prince chuckled. "Members of the diplomatic corps are not chained here. They do get home from time to time. And it's not necessary for you to reside there until you are ready. There is a staff that keeps the cottage year-round, regardless. There will also be easy access to the annual income, because the funds will be deposited in an account for you here."

"For Lord Tentrees, you mean, Your Highness."

"No," the duchess interjected. "It will be in *your* name. This is your property, Kexen. You won't be financially dependent on your husband."

"My goodness." Kexen's mind whirled at the idea of having his own money. "I don't know how I'll manage that."

"You'll get used to it," the duchess said with a quick grin. "I did."

Kexen returned the expression. "Yes, of course." He swallowed hard. "It's all settled then. Please sign the trade agreement, Sir Rolf."

"I will today. And you must busy yourself with getting ready for your wedding and travel. Lord Tentrees' next mission begins in a fortnight, which means you will be married within a week. There's no time to dally."

"A week? My gods. I best get to know my groom quickly, I see. And I need a trousseau. Mistress Camilla will pitch a fit at the rush order. I'm not even sure what I should bring. How does a diplomat's wife dress?"

The duchess rushed to his side. "Not to worry. Remember when I was in this position? You and the seamstress worked wonders for me. We will do the same for you."

Kexen nodded in agreement, yet his mind still reeled with all that had to be done. It was all happening so fast. It scared Kexen as nothing else ever had. But it also excited him. He couldn't wait for his wedding night. He'd saved that one last part of himself for a special man. Now, he would give it to his husband and hope that love would follow.

Chapter Three

Kexen waited for Lord Tentrees to arrive in the duchess' sitting room, of all places. His royal masters were being very kind and treating his upcoming nuptials as if a family marriage were taking place. The familiar and private surroundings helped to ease his nerves a bit, but it was still difficult to keep his ass on the plush cushion of the couch instead of pacing the floor. It wasn't like him to get worked up over anything. He supposed marrying a member of the nobility then being whisked away to a foreign land were reasons enough for his confidence to be tried. At least he'd had time to deal with one worry. He'd found a replacement groomer. Mistress Camilla had graciously agreed that young Henry of the Cooper Village could leave her services and trade up for a most critical court function. Although the boy was young, he'd demonstrated during the ball season that he was someone who met Kexen's exacting standards. His keen eye for fashion rivaled Kexen's own, and he was amenable as well. The duchess had approved the choice already, so that was one less thing to fret over.

A confident rap on the door startled him before he remembered that he had to impress upon his husband-to-be that he was mature enough for the role of Lady Tentrees. Mustering all his courage and straightening his back, he called out, "You may enter."

Whatever his plans to be calm and collected might have been, they flew out of the window the moment his fiancé came through the door. Benedict, Lord Tentrees—*Ben*, he reminded himself—was no less impressive in the light of day than he'd been under the soft lights of the ball. Dressed conservatively in dark brown colors, he still cut a fine figure, his tunic and trousers being form-fitting sufficiently to highlight his strong physique. With his dark hair tied back in a simple queue, his handsome face was on full display. Then he smiled, making Kexen's stomach flip-flop with a combination of renewed nerves and nascent ardor.

Kexen stood on shaky legs. "Lord Tentrees, thank you for calling on me."

"It's Ben, remember?" The gentle admonishment was emphasized with another smile, and when he reached Kexen, he took his hand and planted a soft kiss on the inside of his wrist. "And you have made me the happiest of men by accepting my offer."

Kexen licked his lips. "It was a generous one." Coherent thoughts were difficult given that Ben hadn't released his hand.

"And one that I hope you found appealing on a personal level." Ben maneuvered them so that they sat side by side on the couch, hands still clasped and turned to each other. The feel of the man and his warmth helped to calm Kexen.

Shyness was not an emotion that came naturally to him. At the moment, however, he was finding it hard to look Ben in the eye, and he feared that his cheeks were pinking. "Of course. I remember our encounter very fondly."

"That's good to hear. Sex is certainly an area I wish for us to enjoy together. There is more to marriage than that, though. Please look at me and not the floor." The soft command surprised Kexen. He did as asked and peered into Ben's lovely brown eyes. "Thank you. I much prefer that we deal with each other in a truthful and frank manner. I am sensitive to the differences in our stations, but as my wife, you are entitled to respect and courtesy. And I don't expect blind obedience. If I ask of you something you are uncomfortable with, I want you to tell me."

"I will. I hope you know that you are getting a bride that is perhaps bolder than most." More relaxed now, he offered a coquettish smile and was rewarded when heat came into Ben's eyes.

"I do know, and I like that about you. It will be a handy characteristic for a diplomat's wife." His expression turned a bit serious. "And to that issue, I must discuss something in particular before you order your trousseau...one that I will pay for, just so we're clear on that."

"Yes, Sir Rolf did tell me that you insisted, and I promise to be frugal in my purchasing."

Ben shook his head. "No, you will not. As my wife, you must be outfitted with the finest clothing to see you through the harsh winter of the Iron Shore, as well as stylish and expensive garments for palace life. I have already given Mistress Camilla instructions as such."

That had to have been after he'd spoken to the woman. They'd discussed what outfits he might wear in the style of the duchess that would be practical and versatile. Kexen tried to be circumspect in his glee. The idea of having an unlimited budget to buy clothing delighted him. For once, he'd be working with Mistress Camilla for himself, sorting through patterns and fabrics to suit his tastes. It was a delightful turn of events. "Thank you…Ben. That's very generous of you."

"You are most welcome, although it's a matter of necessity — as are the parameters I've set for your trousseau."

"You want me to dress conservatively." That seemed obvious and something he'd already thought of himself.

"Not necessarily. A little daring is fine. It will catch people's eyes and make us stand out as a couple. The attention will benefit the mission, so long as you don't upstage the queen of the Iron Shore."

"Of course. I understand that issue completely."

"I am not surprised, given your role as a royal groomer…except there is more I would ask of you." Ben hesitated for a moment before continuing. "I want you to wear only women's clothing for the duration of this mission — nothing masculine or even the hybrid style you've set for the duchess."

Surprised, Kexen sat blinking at his future husband like a dimwitted owl before he could muster a response. "You want me to pretend that I am wholly a woman and not the person that I am — someone who is comfortable in the role of either sex and takes pleasure in the clothing attributable to both?"

Ben clasped Kexen's hand with both of his now. "No, my dear. I don't mean that. I will not have us present you as something that you are not. It's merely the window-dressing, if you will." He paused a moment more. "The new queen is young, ascending the throne early in her life because of her father's sudden and accidental death while hunting. She is rumored to be a principled woman, yet a bit capricious and having lusty appetites. She's enjoying an array of lovers before settling down with a consort. It is said that no unmarried man in her court is safe, and I, for one, do not intend to conduct diplomacy by using my body."

"But you will be married," Kexen ventured, not understanding whatever political subtly his fiancé was providing. "Does she poach on other women's territory, and even if she does, surely she will not tie her decision about the treaty to your willingness to warm her bed?"

Ben grimaced. "She does seem to have drawn for herself that one line…not as you say, '*poaching on a legally binding arrangement*'. I would agree, as well, based on what I know of her that she won't decide who gets the treaty purely based on who pleasures her the best and most, but I'm not as convinced that an ego bruised by rejection might not prove an influence.

"I'm also not certain that her sense of morals will view a male wife as the same barrier as a woman. To my knowledge, her people have never sanctioned such a marriage, and my hope is that if you are at least clothed as a woman, it will stay any impulses she may have so that I need not find myself having to rebuff her." The man sighed as he added, "I could be wrong about all this, but my diplomatic instincts are excellent, and the outcome of this mission is too important. Moorcondia needs iron ore, and maintaining the supply from the best known source in the world is going to be critical. If the new queen decides to supply only Far Isle, it will put us at a distinct power disadvantage. Can you do this for me?" he added with an intense look.

Kexen understood the importance of their success. And he was not so taken by Ben's soft tone and open face that he truly thought this was a question so much as a command. There was really only one acceptable answer, and he supposed he should appreciate the gentleness in which the order had been couched. It boded well that the man wasn't going to wield his power with brute force. Besides, it might be fun to dress only in gowns for the few months that the mission would last. He would accept it as a lark and a challenge to his skills with clothing, makeup and hairstyling.

He smiled at Ben. "Of course. I want to be as much help as I can for you and your mission. I will go see Mistress Camilla right away and get started on choosing the right ensembles. That is, of course, once we are done here," he added, batting his eyes. It would be nice to enjoy a bit of naughtiness with his fiancé. There was no harm in it, certainly.

But Ben disappointed him in that regard. Rising and tugging Kexen to his feet, he planted a quick kiss on the back of Kexen's hand. "I will leave you to it, my darling. You are a temptation, to be sure, but I must insist that we observe proprieties until we wed." Then he chuckled. "Now, now, Kexen, no pouting."

"Sorry." He hadn't realized he'd let his disappointment show.

"No apology needed. I am flattered, but our big day is near, and I can't wait to make you mine."

The look Ben gave him made Kexen flush and his cock stirred instantly to full hardness. It made him wish for the wedding to come even sooner. He couldn't wait to become Lady Tentrees and have Ben claim him in the one way no man ever had.

* * * *

Kexen felt as if he'd walked through a dream as he entered his husband's apartment. *Oh, that word sounds so strange. I have a* husband. It had been like that the whole day as he'd dressed for his wedding, then went through the ceremony that bound him for life to the man who'd stood beside him. His life didn't seem real to him. It had all been glorious, though, with a lovely feast afterward hosted by Prince Soren and the Duchess of Vostguard. The royal couples' generosity still stunned him. What he'd done with and for his master had been based on loyalty and affection. To his mind, there had been no question that he would remain steadfast to the man and face any trouble he did. Kexen hadn't expected or needed any tangible appreciation for it. This had been an amazing day, however, and the way in which the prince and duchess had treated him as if he were one of their own had taken some of the sting out of his family being unable to make the journey in time. Ben had promised they would visit both of their families once they returned from their hopefully successful mission. Kexen was determined to make it so. He wanted to please Ben and aid his country.

Ben ushered Kexen farther into the sitting room by placing his hand against the small of Kexen's back. Even with the thickness of his cape acting as a barrier between them, he could feel the effect of Ben's touch. With their wedding night fast approaching, Kexen's anticipation had reached a nearly intolerable level. *I want him to claim me, now.* With the feasting done and darkness having fallen, it would come soon enough. They'd have a few days, as well, to become close to each other until they had to set sail. He pictured them spending the entire time in bed, a lovely fantasy, during which they explored each other's bodies and came in all the various ways possible. They would talk, too, of course, given how little time there'd been for them to get acquainted. The wedding and preparations for the voyage had taken up a great deal of both their attentions. His experience so far gave him hope that he and Benedict, Lord Tentrees, would suit very well. And while he knew that his husband would be taken away to tend to the business of the mission over the next few days, he harbored hope that he could be a little stingy with him.

An older man and woman stood at attention near the far doorway. Kexen had met them both, although his new lady's maid hadn't yet started her duties. Henry had dressed him earlier in the day with the duchess overseeing the effort. The turn-around in their roles had made them both laugh. Poor Henry had been caught in the middle, trying to do his job while his two masters acted like giddy girls. It was a memory Kexen would cherish his whole life. He still wore the lavish white silk and lace gown that had been yet another gift from the royal couple. Ben had given him a choice in attire for the ceremony. Kexen had chosen to dress as a woman because it felt right to start his marriage as they had agreed he'd go on to maintain during the mission. And he was actually looking forward to presenting purely as female. He'd spent long stretches of his life dressed as a male without ever compromising on who he was inside. This would make for an interesting change, and he expected to have no trouble separating his outside appearance from what lived inside his head and heart. He'd always known his true self, and this time would be no different.

Ben stopped him in front of the servants. "Euphemia, Baldrick, I present to you Lady Tentrees."

Although Kexen had already been addressed by his new title since the wedding, hearing it in this domestic environment somehow made it all the more real. Both people bowed and murmured congratulations. Before anything more could be said, there was a sharp rap on the outer door. Ben turned with a frown. "Come in."

A man entered with a serious look on his face. He was wearing the livery of the foreign minister. "Pardon the intrusion, my lord. I have an urgent message from the crown."

Ben's expression grew stern. "Of course. Go to the public drawing room downstairs. I'll join you after I've seen my wife settled." The other man left quickly, leaving Kexen with a feeling of unease. But Ben smiled at him as he said, "Please let Euphemia ready you to retire. I promise to join you shortly." There was a reassurance in his gaze, as well, something more intimate that eased Kexen.

He let a bit of coquettishness shine through. Soon it would be only the two of them. "I hope so." He watched his husband leave before untying his cape. "Let us not dawdle, Euphemia. I don't want to keep my husband waiting, but I fear I'm in need of a quick bath." Once again nerves warred with anticipation. Hopefully a soak in warm water would blunt one and enhance the other. Then he couldn't wait to see the look on Ben's face when he saw him in the beautiful and sexy lace dressing gown that he'd chosen. A blushing bride would wear a nightgown underneath. That wasn't Kexen's style, however. He would be naked.

* * * *

Ben ran a hand down his face as he took in the grave news from the minister's messenger. "Those sneaky bastards," he said when the man had finished. "I should have known that the envoy from Far Isle would jump the time for arrival. And he's already disembarked, you say?"

The man nodded curtly. "Based on the timing of his departure from his native land, we have to assume so, my lord."

"Damnation." He pondered his next move, the obvious one needing little thought. "Well, we can do nothing about his head start, but we will cut his time alone with Queen Amira short. Can the captain ready the ship for a departure tonight?"

"He was my first stop, my lord, and the answer is yes. He waits only for your arrival and the next high tide."

"And when is that?"

The man grimaced. "Within the hour, my lord. I'm sorry for the rush, given that it's your wedding night."

Ben waved away that concern. "It's not ideal, but my wife and I both understand the needs of Moorcondia come first. Please tell the captain we will come on board shortly."

"Yes, my lord."

Ben followed the messenger out of the room, turning toward the stairs that led to the floor housing his apartment. As he took the steps two at a time, his mind whirled with the details of how he could make ready to leave that night. He couldn't afford to wait even half a day for the tide to turn again in their favor for setting sail. As much as he hated the idea, the consummation of his wedding would have to be a quick affair. He simply didn't have the luxury anymore of seducing his bride as he'd intended to. Thank the gods Kexen was an experienced man. They could achieve the necessary formalities easily enough, then explore each other more thoroughly during the many-day journey on the ship. His cock responded enthusiastically to both ideas. The stress of the hasty departure wasn't going to impede his ability to claim his bride.

Baldrick was waiting for him in the sitting room. Ben tore off his coat while quickly explaining the situation and what needed to be done. He didn't wait to see if Baldrick was acting on his orders before heading into the bedroom. He had no doubt about his manservant's ability to pack for him on such short notice. Euphemia would do the same for Kexen, although the trousseau was mostly tucked away in trunks already, having never been unpacked since its arrival from the palace. When he passed through the doorway, he was momentarily stunned at the sight of his bride with his hair hanging in soft waves around his beautiful face. He wore a white dressing gown, frothy with lace, and sufficiently sheer that he could glimpse the enticing package that lay under it.

As pressed for time as he was, he couldn't help stopping in his tracks to drink in the sight of Kexen. His arousal bloomed fully, his dick rising as much as its cramped confines would allow. He could feel the blood pounding there, and his whole body flushed with heat. Perhaps it was a good thing that they had to act in haste. He wasn't sure he would be able to rein his passion in to make slow love to his new wife as he deserved. That thought appalled the controlled and civilized part of him, but his primitive side embraced the idea.

The presence of the maid caught his attention. He'd been so absorbed in drinking in the sight of Kexen that he'd quite forgotten they wouldn't be alone. "Euphemia, go see Baldrick for your new orders." He didn't take his gaze off his bride as he said it. "And shut the door behind you." That last order was perhaps unnecessary. Anyone with sight likely could tell what his plans were, even if it weren't his wedding night.

The soft sound of the latch as Euphemia closed them into the bedroom was sufficient to move him into action. Without saying another word, he strode to his bride and swept him into an embrace. The moment their lips touched, Ben released his passion, claiming his wife's mouth possessively. With a soft moan, Kexen let Ben's tongue inside. As Ben claimed that small part of him, he crushed their bodies together, groaning at the delightful friction of his cock against an equally hard Kexen. He walked them closer to the bed as he roamed his hands around his bride. As thin as it was, the dressing gown nevertheless provided too much of a frustrating barrier. He plucked the ribbon tied around Kexen's waist and opened it. Now he was able to caress all that silky skin, from his wife's small pecs to his tight ass. Ben cupped and squeezed every bit of it, leaving no space between them. He wanted more, however. He wanted to see.

Breaking away, he slipped the gown off his bride's shoulder and allowed it to pool at their feet. He smiled at his lovely wife and took in the full sight of him, from the flushed cheeks to the erect and slender cock. "You are a vision, my darling."

Kexen dropped his gaze in a fetchingly shy manner. "You have me at a disadvantage, my lord. I can hardly see you at all."

Ben started to undo his belt before remembering the need for haste and reaching for the ties of his trousers instead. There was no time to do more than free that necessary part of himself. "I am sorry, darling, but our plans have changed. Far Isle is playing dirty, as we feared they might. When you know little about your adversary, it's best to expect the worse from them. We must leave within the hour." His hard dick sprang free, and he tucked the hem of his tunic inside his belt in order to leave his cock unimpeded.

Kexen gratifyingly homed his gaze onto the sight of it and licked his lips. "Oh, my lord. You are even larger than I remembered."

Ben took a step toward him. "Not too much so, I hope."

Kexen giggled. "Is there such a thing?" Then he sobered. "I'm sorry. What are you saying? Must we forego our wedding night?"

Ben took his bride's face between his hands and kissed him. "Certainly not. We must consummate our marriage so that there is no question of it being binding. Regrettably, it has to be done before we start our journey. I will take no chances of anything interfering with your claim to being my wife."

He kissed Kexen again as he walked him to the side of the bed, then turned him around. That perfect rump beckoned him. He slid one finger down the crack to tease the hole within. "I'd intended to spend the whole night exploring you from head to toe, but time is not on our side. I will make it as good as I can for you, under the circumstances."

A hitch in Kexen's breath was all the response he got as Ben turned him once more to lift him onto the edge of the bed. Then Ben splayed Kexen's legs, enjoying the feel of the silky skin and the sight of the clipped hair surrounding an erect cock. Clasping the underside of the boy's thighs, he exposed the puckered ring nestled inside his ass cheeks. The vision was so compelling that he felt an almost overwhelming urge to breach it immediately. Sanity prevailed, however, and he looked at the nightstand to see if it held what he needed. Of course, it did. Baldrick knew well how to provision his master. He slicked two fingers with oil while holding Kexen in place with the other hand. Reaching for his bride's hole, he swirled around it before sliding past its entrance. His fingers were enveloped by sweetly warm tightness that softened almost immediately in welcome to his intrusion. He would have loved to explore that place, slowly opening it even more for his cock, but he didn't have the luxury of such tender ministrations.

Thrusting deeply, he rotated his hand in order to stroke Kexen's prostate. It was the quickest way to make a man ready for him that he'd found. His bride rewarded him with breathy gasps while clutching at the bedding. The flesh clasping his fingers loosened even more as he quickly fucked Kexen's channel. At the same time, he clasped Kexen's dick with his other hand and jerked it with the same rhythm and speed. Pre-cum welled up in his bride's slit, testament that Ben's efforts were having the necessary effect. When Kexen seemed sufficiently receptive, Ben proceeded to the final act of claiming. He doused his dick in oil, his hands almost shaking from need and not caring if he stained the carpet. He could always replace it, but this first time with his bride would remain a unique event. The urgency in him was far more than the obligation to start his journey soon. Although he wasn't going to be Kexen's first, he would be his last, gods willing. Ben would do everything in his power to ensure a long life together, but for now, he simply had to get inside his bride.

Positioning his cock at the entrance of Kexen's hole, he bared his thoughts as he rarely did. "I have never wanted anyone more."

He kept his eyes open, because he wanted the vision of his bride being claimed by him the first time to become fixed in his memory. As he pressed past the ring, that tightness he'd first felt was back, only now the channel was being challenged by something much larger than his fingers. There was no turning back, however, so he pushed past the resistance, slowly yet steadily, sure that Kexen knew how to accept his cock and would relax to take it in. That didn't happen, and Kexen's beautiful face scrunched up—not in passion, but in obvious pain. Ben clutched his bride's cock, which had flagged somewhat, and jerked it with quick, sure strokes to bring it back to full hardness. He kept up the effort as he continued to push inside Kexen's ass. And as he landed balls deep, he realized too late the reality of the situation.

He's a virgin. No, that couldn't be. Everyone in the palace knew of the boy's exploits. He was free with his favors. Surely Ben's cock wasn't the first to make this journey. Yet as he began to fuck his bride, the truth was etched on the boy's face. The way in which Kexen's body resisted him was obvious now, as well. There was nothing to be done about it, except bring them both to a quick conclusion. Ben redoubled his efforts, glad when Kexen squirmed from a climax. The sight of his bride's cum spurting to coat his hand sent Ben over the edge, too. He thrust in as deep as he could and emptied himself inside his wife.

For long seconds, the only sounds in the room were their harsh breathing as they recovered from their mutual orgasms. Ben used the time to ponder what he could possibly say to excuse his blunder. Words were central to his career, yet he couldn't muster anything that sounded other than trite to him. He decided not to even try, using actions to speak for him. When his breath was sufficiently recovered, he eased out of his bride and hurried into the bathing room. There he soaked a washcloth, and he returned to find Kexen just as he'd left him — except that the boy's eyes were open and he was staring at the ceiling. Ben went to him and began the process of cleaning up the mess he'd made — both physically and emotionally.

"My dear, I cannot tell you how sorry I am." He started with wiping Kexen's stomach and groin of the boy's own spending. "I had thought you experienced. Had I known you were a virgin, I would have gone more slowly." He moved onto Kexen's hole, relieved to find the area rather red and swollen but not torn or bleeding. *Small comfort.*

When he was finished, he tossed the cloth, unheeding of where it landed, in order to help his bride to sit up on the edge of the bed. Kexen didn't look at him, so Ben bent to try to catch his eye. "Are you all right?" Somewhat of a moronic question, but he remained dumbfounded as to the right words to use.

Kexen's shoulders moved on a deep breath, then the air came out in a noticeable shudder. "I was saving myself for someone special." He looked at Ben now with a guarded expression. "For my husband, as it turned out."

Ben cupped the boy's face, grateful that he didn't shy away. "I apologize unreservedly. I have proven to be a poor husband only hours after our ceremony. Can you forgive me?" He held his breath waiting for the answer. It was entirely possible that his bride would rightly reject him for this blunder. An unusual feeling crept over him — dread.

Kexen lifted his chin. "There is nothing to forgive, my lord. Your mission requires haste, so we must not waste any more time with this. Thank you for cleaning me. Please send Euphemia in so that I may dress for our journey."

Ben should have been relieved, but his bride's expression belayed his words. He would be a poor diplomat indeed not to be able to read other people's feelings. His wife was hurt and angry…and rightly so. Their marriage was off to a rocky start, but he could fix this. It would take time, but they had over a week's journey by sea. He'd take the opportunity to woo his bride properly. All would be well.

It had to be — and for reasons that he realized had nothing to do with the mission.

Chapter Four

Kexen stood as still as he could while Euphemia buttoned his gray leather gloves, unsure that his own hands were steady enough to do so. He was grateful, as well, that the woman was frugal with her words. He didn't think he could bear any cheery banter about his wedding and the trip he was about to embark on with his husband. *Ben*. His dream man's claiming of him made Kexen truly question whether he'd made a profound mistake. Gone was the considerate person he'd come to know over the last few days. In his place was a driven diplomat who seemed callous to anything but his professional ambition. Kexen had barely understood the need for an urgent consummation before he'd found himself on his back, his legs spread. Even then he hadn't realized there would be nearly no chance to acclimate himself to the invasion of another man's cock before it had happened.

He stared at his reflection in the nearby long mirror once Euphemia was finished. What he saw was a pale person dressed in layers of dove gray. He'd chosen the simple traveling dress that he would wear to embark on his journey to the Iron Shore the previous day. It had looked so lovely with his cloak of a deeper shade lined with fox fur. Now the entire ensemble reflected his mood, despite how his matching fur hat sat rakishly on his head while his simple braid of hair hung over his shoulder. The look did nothing to change his dark demeanor. He was as beautiful as he'd hoped, yet he felt nothing of the kind. His reflection showed only a sad, little Outer Vale boy bracing against suddenly strong emotional winds beyond his control. He lacked the strength to overcome it at the moment. If nothing else, the ache deep inside his ass from his brutal deflowering reminded him steadily that his marriage was already on the rocks, and he couldn't muster the energy to pretend otherwise.

I can simply leave. The sudden thought startled him. It was true, though. For the first time in his life, he had his own money and being married meant that Rolf had no control over him anymore. No one did, unless one counted his husband. But the law didn't give a man that much dominion over his wife. If Kexen wanted, he could walk away and make his home in that astounding freehold that was now his. Ben would be unable to stop him — except that would also nullify the trade agreement, and Kexen couldn't be so selfish. His family would benefit greatly from it, which in turn would help his sisters and cousins making more advantageous matches of their own. He had no right to destroy that. Besides, he was no coward. Only a few hours ago, he'd pledged himself to Ben. Kexen was a man of honor and would keep those vows. He could only hope that Ben's promise to make things up to him would prove to be more than mere words.

Kexen turned away from the mirror. "I'm ready." Accepting the fur muff Euphemia handed him, he steeled himself to go meet his husband outside.

The freezing night announced that winter had truly arrived. It would be worse down by the docks where their ship awaited them. Kexen was glad for the warm clothing he had on and shoved his hands inside the muff as he descended the front steps to join his husband by the carriage that would convey them. He didn't return Ben's smile, nor did he take the hand that was proffered. He merely allowed the man to take hold of his elbow and guide him up and into the closed interior of the carriage. Ben joined him on the opposite bench, shut the door and rapped for the driver to start. Kexen huddled against the plush velvet of his tufted seat, keeping his gaze downcast and trying not to show the discomfort that sitting caused.

Ben wasn't fooled. "Are you in much pain?"

"I'm fine." Kexen didn't care about his curtness. Inside the muff, he rubbed his thumb against the filigreed gold band lying under the glove. He tried to remind himself about the joy he'd felt when Ben had slipped it on his finger, as well as his sense of pride when he'd done the same for the man, giving him a simple masculine band. It had been wonderful to be able to buy it with his own money.

"My dear, I thought we'd agreed to be honest with each other."

Kexen couldn't help grimacing, but he did look at his husband as he answered. "Did we? I don't recall. But I am being so, regardless. You seem to have forgotten that I was raised as a boy, and as such, I've suffered far worse hurts in my rough and tumble childhood. Don't let the female garb you require me to wear fool you into thinking that I'm delicate—not that women are, anyway," he added in a murmur. His cousin Adela could probably take Ben down in a fight if she put her mind to it. Picturing her doing so gave him momentary, if not guilty, pleasure.

Ben sighed but wisely didn't try to reach for him. "I didn't mean physically so much as—"

"You're worried that I'm upset?" Kexen spat out. Demureness was never his forte. Really, it was surprising that he'd kept up the pretense for so long. "Angry? *Disillusioned*? Perhaps I should resent the fact that you assumed me to be such a slut that you'd be traveling a well-worn path that needed no gentleness."

Ben winced at Kexen's harsh words. He looked so contrite that Kexen almost took them back and apologized. Almost. But he held his tongue because if he didn't focus on his resentment, he feared he'd burst into tears—and that would be too mortifying for words. "Don't give it another thought. The mission comes first. I understood what I was getting into by marrying you." That wasn't true, naturally. He'd painted romantic pictures of what it would be like married to a diplomat. The harsh reality of how his feelings would have to take second place to Ben's duty was sinking in. Kexen had always been a quick study. He could adapt, and pride alone dictated that he not let even his husband see the depth of his disappointment.

"I will make this up to you," Ben said in a quiet voice. "Once we're settled in our berth on the ship, and if you permit me, I will show you how good it can be between us."

Hope had always lived strong in him. Kexen tried to ignore the effect of Ben's words. His cock proved to be either stupider or smarter than his brain, because it rose at the sound of his husband's promise. Kexen bit the inside of his cheek to dissuade it. "If you say so." He would forgive Ben, eventually. There was no point in staying in a marriage lacking sex and being at odds with his husband. But he wasn't going to make it easy on the man. Ben had a lot to prove to his bride. Kexen would demand no less.

The docks to the great lake of Moorcondia being at the farthest point from the back of the palace, it was a longer journey than he'd expected. He'd never had cause to come to this part of Moorcondia before, and he took in his surroundings with unabashed curiosity as Ben helped him down from the carriage and led him over to the gangplank. A burly man in a sharp, black uniform and full beard waited for them, his hands clasped behind his back. This was obviously the captain of the ship they'd be traveling on. His expression was banked and respectful. He nodded at Ben as they arrived. "My lord. Welcome to the *Morning Star*."

"Thank you, captain. The king appreciates your alacrity in readying on such short notice."

"I serve at his pleasure…and yours. If there is anything I can do to make your time on my ship more pleasant, please let me know."

"Thank you." Ben motioned with his free hand at Kexen. "This is my wife."

The captain trained his gaze on Kexen. If he thought there was anything unusual in his other passenger, he didn't show it. "My lady."

"Captain." Kexen was as cordial as his current emotions permitted. The last thing he wanted was to make another person uncomfortable. Poor Baldrick and Euphemia would be unavoidable collateral damage in his marriage strife, of course. That couldn't be helped as they knew all the intimate details. Kexen was resolved, however, to keep everyone else ignorant of his dirty laundry.

The captain shouted over his shoulder. "Boy, come escort Lord and Lady Tentrees to their berth."

A lad not much younger than Kexen came trotting down the gangplank and waved them on. "If you please, my lord, my lady."

As they walked up to the ship, Kexen appreciated that Ben still had a hold on him. It was steeper than he would have expected, and the dark, churning water below them appeared menacing, as if it were just waiting for a misstep so that it could swallow them up. A stiff wind made him glad once more of his warm clothing, but the way their wooden path swayed made his head swim a bit and his stomach turn.

Ben's grip on his hand tightened. "I have you."

The hold and the reassuring words, uttered as they were in Ben's kind yet confident tone, eased Kexen's worry. He felt safe but also irritated that it took so little for him to soften toward his husband. His pique came out once they'd settled on the deck by his letting go of Ben's hand and stuffing his own back into the muff. If Ben was hurt by the gesture, he didn't show it. There were steep stairs leading down into the bowels of the ship and everything smelled of fish, tar and some other unidentifiable and unpleasant odors. While Kexen knew that his country benefited from ships traveling the trade route and that passengers often went along simply for the adventure, he wasn't sure he'd like this mode of travel for himself. He certainly couldn't imagine it being fun. His body was making ominous objections to the way the ship swayed, even while at dock.

Their berth, though, was surprisingly roomy, which helped with the sudden anxiety of being cooped up. The ship rocked to one side suddenly enough that Kexen started to tumble over. Once again, Ben was there, grabbing hold and grounding him by his side. It was a nice, warm place to be, and Kexen gave himself a few seconds to bask in it before remembering how mad he was. He pulled away, bracing his feet to keep his balance. Ben opened his mouth, then shut it again when there was a knock at the door. They both stood aside while Baldrick and Euphemia came in, lugging the traveling bags that held what they would need for the voyage. The space got more cramped with four people in it, but he was glad to see that their servants would be sleeping elsewhere, at least. There was only the one bed, however, for him and Ben. Kexen studiously avoided looking at it.

Ben took his leave once the luggage was settled to speak to the captain about...something. If he'd said exactly what, Kexen hadn't been paying attention. It was none of his affair what these powerful men spoke about. All he wanted was privacy and the chance to strip out of his clothing. As lovely as his outfit was, it weighed on him, not only because the cumulative material was heavy but also because from this day forward, he was bound to live as a woman. With the restriction forced upon him after his recent experience, dressing in traditionally women's garments felt like a burden, not a naughty adventure. It now somehow made him vulnerable in a way he'd never experienced before—maybe simply because they hampered his movement. *I can't run or defend myself as easily.* That was a strange worry. He wasn't afraid of Ben, after all...merely hurt and angry. Besides, he reminded himself that he'd packed some male attire just in case, although he wasn't sure what the 'in case' really meant.

Before Ben had shut the door behind him, he'd bidden Kexen to settle in for the night. He'd heard an order in those words and immediately bristled, which was stupid, because he was weary from the day and sliding into bed — alone, at least for a while — was appealing. And there was emotional relief when he was alone with his maid. Euphemia began the process of undressing him without being told. She was efficient, but Kexen still chafed at having to wait for the woman to do everything for him. Having been the Duchess of Vostguard's personal groomer, he hadn't really appreciated how tedious it was to be waited on, especially when dealing with churning emotions that demanded privacy to process.

Soon, though, he was tucked into bed, wearing a warm nightgown that was meant to be serviceable, not enticing. That suited him just fine. When he pictured Ben joining him in what was essentially a wooden box with a mattress, it would be a snug fit. It was hard to imagine, too, what pleasure could be had on their journey. The idea of being breached again held little appeal. Naturally, he wasn't going to deny Ben his rights entirely. He just needed time, that was all. Hopefully, the many-days' journey would give them an opportunity to make right what had gone so wrong in their marriage. Ben would understand, as well, that Kexen needed time to recover from the first invasion. It was a good excuse to explore each other in ways that Kexen was more comfortable with. That thought eased his mind, and, with the emotional and physically demanding day taking its toll, he had no trouble falling asleep.

* * * *

Ben entered the cabin as quietly as he could, leaving Baldrick behind. He didn't want to risk waking his wife for something as simple as undressing himself. The day had been a long one, and if he was dead on his feet, Kexen had to be even more so. *Especially after what I did to him.* He cringed each time he remembered how he'd hurt his bride for want of more care. He'd been so focused on the mission that he hadn't given the right consideration to what he was doing. It was unforgiveable. Well, he hoped that was not so. Married life would be a horror if he couldn't convince Kexen to give him another chance. And it was up to him, not Kexen, to make amends. The boy's fury and hurt over the event were justified, because the accusation that he'd assumed Kexen to be an experienced person was true, not that he'd thought the word *slut* or any other derogatory description. But he *had* thought Kexen to be more adventurous with his previous lovers than he'd been, and that was the problem. He should have taken the time to find out. The speed with which they'd had to act was no excuse. Ben would do better from now on, no matter how pressing his duties became.

An oil lamp that was bolted to the ceiling burned low, casting the room in an almost romantic glow. Kexen lay curled on his side, his back against the wall, one hand fisted under his chin. For the first time, Ben was seeing him without artifice and entirely vulnerable. Gone was the sophisticated flirt. With his hair in a messy braid and no paint on his face, he looked impossibly young. Ben had made a stupid mistake allowing Kexen's outward confidence to blind him to the fact that his bride remained a boy from the country.

He needed and deserved protection, kindness and patience. It was up to Ben to woo him, show him how good lovemaking could be between them. He vowed to go slowly. They had a long journey ahead of them, plenty of time to get to know one another and for him to rebuild trust with his wife.

Ben had to brace his legs against a sudden lurch of the ship. They were barely out of port and already the lake waters were rough. That wasn't surprising, given what the captain had told him. Winter was coming early and fast everywhere, including to the Iron Shore. It was a good thing the Far Isle envoy had upped the timetable, as it happened, and perhaps it was the weather that had caused the man to leave on his mission early. He might prove as honorable and straight-forward as Ben was himself. They were diplomatic adversaries, but they didn't have to be enemies. There was no value in looking for trouble, either, although being ready for it at all times was a must.

The journey would only become more treacherous once they reached the open sea. Crossing it would be difficult, and soon the passage northward would become nearly impossible, once the storms picked up and the waters started to freeze. Even far from shore, ice floes lurked beneath the surface waiting to wreck any ship that came their way. Ben felt excitement at starting his mission regardless and was confident that he could turn a winter trapped on the Iron Shore into diplomatic success. And he was a good sailor, so he didn't mind the tossing and turning. He frowned at a sudden thought that he hadn't asked Kexen if he was experienced with voyaging by boat. *Likely not*. Pleasure trips on ships like this were a rare pastime. As someone from the Outer Vale, he'd probably done no more than putter around a small lake in a rowboat.

Ben put aside the worry and quickly stripped off his clothing. Baldrick had left him a warm nightshirt, and while he usually slept nude, the chill in the room dissuaded him from that habit. Although he didn't want to wake Kexen, he knew that was really no way to prevent it. Or perhaps his wife was a sound sleeper and wouldn't stir, even with Ben's climbing into bed. His cock stirred at the thought of joining the boy. He pressed the heel of his palm against it as a warning. He wasn't going to try to do anything more than sleep. If his wife happened to snuggle against him, however, it would be a welcome thing. He liked the idea of simply holding Kexen in his arms.

Ben turned the flame of the lamp down even more, not intending to put the room in total darkness. He didn't want to risk Kexen waking up disorientated. With his gaze fixed on his wife, Ben padded over to the bed and eased himself down on the edge. The moment his ass hit the mattress, Kexen's face scrunched up and he murmured something before his eyes fluttered open. When the boy saw him, there was a clear moment of near panic, making Ben's heart sink. The last thing he wanted was for his wife to fear him. Anger was preferable, but even as he searched for some soothing words to utter, his wife's eyes went wide and he bolted upright.

Ben jumped to his feet and held his hands out. "My dear, everything is fine. Please don't be alarmed. I merely seek to sleep beside you."

His words didn't help. Kexen's expression grew worse. Then he clamped his hand over his mouth as he scrambled out from under the covers. Before Ben could realize what was happening, his bride fell to the floor, grabbed the chamber pot tied to the bed post and vomited whatever was left from their lovely wedding feast. As Ben hurried to help, holding Kexen's hair back and running a palm down the boy's back, he understood that their wedding night disaster was the least of their worries. They hadn't yet left the lake and his poor bride was already seasick.

Ben stayed with Kexen until the last of the heaving abated, then fetched a cup of water. "Take a little to rinse out your mouth." He waited while Kexen did as advised before helping him back into bed. After tucking his shivering body in, Ben said, "My poor darling, I'm sorry for this. Traveling by water does this to many people. The good news is that you'll settle down in a few days at most and won't suffer this terrible sickness anymore."

Kexen gave him a dubious look before closing his eyes. Ben soothed him as best he could by stroking his hair. Once Kexen's breathing evened out, Ben slipped in beside him. His plan was already in jeopardy, yet he remained optimistic. He'd never known seasickness to afflict someone for long. Hopefully, his bride would recover quickly and be receptive to his attention. In the meantime, he would take care of him himself as a good husband should. With his plan revised and fixed in his head, he let the day's exhaustion claim him.

* * * *

"It's beautiful in a haunting sort of way."

Ben gripped his wife's waist tighter before answering. As it made its final approach to the dock, the ship was being buffeted by churning waves and wind almost as much as it had been out at sea. It was not surprising, given that the Iron Shore was a coastal country hemmed in on three sides and with nothing shielding it from the ocean. "Yes, it is."

He'd seen sketched pictures of the Iron Shore, naturally, as part of his preparation for the mission. They didn't do it justice, though. The entire country, which was no bigger than the Moorcondian capital city, was constructed out of a blindingly white stone that rose in layers against a backdrop of the formidable and iron-rich mountains, which gave the country its name. With the heavy snow cover, the buildings blended into its surroundings. And at the top, the palace gleamed, appearing as if it were a magical place rising to the clouds that one could never truly reach. *Such whimsical thoughts. It's the lack of sleep. I know better than to attribute airy fantasy to a place where one needs to tread lightly.*

It was the effect of the journey and the torture it had inflicted upon Kexen. That first night had been the start of a never-ending bout of severe seasickness. Ben's prediction of a quick recovery had proven to be entirely wrong. The poor boy had never found his sea legs, keeping little down and worrying Ben and their servants alike. Euphemia had dosed Kexen with some herbal remedies and salty broth to little avail. They had resorted to relocating Kexen as much as possible to the deck where the fresh, brisk air and the ability to see the horizon helped somewhat. The mounting cold had made that remedy problematic for other reasons, so there had been a constant back and forth. Ben had carried his bride as much as possible, because Kexen had grown very weak from lack of sustenance. His beautiful cheeks were hollowed from his loss of weight — as if the boy had had any fat to spare — and his skin was nearly as pale as the Iron Shore stone. Their arrival was a relief, to say the least. Now, Ben had to navigate his visit alone until his wife had recovered enough to join him. He was anxious to get him settled as quickly as possible.

"I'm sorry I've been such a bother. You don't need me to worry about." Kexen's voice was thin and breathless.

"Please don't fret over that, my darling." The one positive thing to come out of Kexen's sickness was that they had spent nearly every moment of the journey together. There had been little talking, given the circumstances, but Ben had read to his wife to take his mind off things, as well as simply keeping him company. It had been gratifying that Kexen seemed to prefer him playing nursemaid over Euphemia doing so. And of course, there had been no possibility of anything sexual between them. The pressure to rectify the debacle of their wedding night had been taken away by unforeseen circumstances, allowing them time to get to know each other. He wouldn't have wished his wife to be so miserable, but there was a silver lining in the situation.

"I should have a few hours to rest before whatever welcoming banquet they have planned. I promise I won't faint."

Ben couldn't help smiling. His wife had admirable fortitude. "You will spend the rest of the day and night in bed. I will make your excuses, and no one should be surprised that you aren't up for socializing after such a rough journey. Hopefully your appetite and strength will return quickly, so that you can be presented to the queen tomorrow night. There is no argument on this," he added when he sensed Kexen was ready to balk.

"Your health is paramount. Queen Amira will understand. There will be a long winter for you to dazzle her and her court. I want you in fit shape, as I expect this will be a tense mission."

There was no more talking as the ship slid alongside a long pier. Sailors jumped off to secure the lines. As soon as the captain gave them permission to disembark, Ben led Kexen carefully down the gangplank. It was a tricky thing, watching both their steps and the arrival of a retinue of mounted guards followed by an open carriage and an empty supply wagon. Everything was white on white with only black trim on both men and beasts, as well as the vehicles, to break up the monotone. The starkness was eye-catching, and it made him wonder if the Iron Shore people used any other color at all. Knowing that they had to import their horses, it was an impressive display of wealth. He couldn't help wondering if the Far Isle envoy had received a similar welcome.

Now, now, mustn't be petty.

A man dressed more elaborately than the others jumped off his horse and strode forward to greet them. He sketched a deep bow before speaking. "Lord Tentrees, welcome to Queen Amira's Iron Shore. I am Master Prime Minister." He smiled, showing a row of bright teeth. Somehow the expression didn't seem sincere, and Ben put him mentally on the list of people to watch out for.

Unsurprised, though, that the queen's man was not entirely to be trusted, Ben ignored his impression for the present and nodded his head. "Master Prime Minister, thank you for your welcome. I present my wife, Lady Tentrees."

"Madam." If the minister saw anything unusual in Kexen, he was careful not to show it.

"Master Prime Minister." Kexen's voice sounded stronger, and he straightened in Ben's hold.

Ben took a moment to feel pride over his wife's strength, but he wasn't going to let politics take any more of a toll on him than it had during the voyage. "Master Prime Minister, if you could please see us to our quarters as quickly as possible. My wife suffered greatly of seasickness during the journey."

"Of course. This way, please. We have a carriage to convey you." He turned to walk back to his retinue. Stopping beside the vehicle, he added, "I hope its open structure isn't a problem. We of the Iron Shore embrace winter whenever we can."

Kexen answered before Ben had a chance to. "I expect the cold air will be bracing."

With no further comment, Ben helped his wife into the lush conveyance and tucked the thick blanket waiting for them over his lap. With a crack of the reins, the coachman got them moving. The mounted soldiers formed an escort around them, which hopefully was simply for the pomp of it all and not because danger lurked on their journey through the city. It was impossible to tell, either way. Unlike Moorcondians, the Iron Shore people seemed unimpressed with foreign visitors. Those they passed as the carriage climbed up the stone street barely acknowledged them. That was perhaps all to the good. Kexen leaned against him more heavily as the journey continued. He really needed to get his wife into a bed that didn't rock constantly. When they reached their destination, Ben helped Kexen out of the carriage and eyed the steep steps to the double-doored entrance. He made his decision in a heartbeat, sweeping his bride into his arms before beginning the ascent. The poor boy was light, even with the voluminous skirts and thick cloak.

On a gasp, Kexen wrapped his arms around Ben's neck. "This isn't necessary."

"I beg to differ." To prove his point, Ben picked up his pace so that he was already setting Kexen onto his feet before the Master Prime Minister had gone halfway up the stairs. Ben smiled brightly at the man. "The Iron Shore is even more beautiful than it appears at a distance."

The Master Prime Minister acknowledged him with a nod of his head. "You are too kind, my lord. Please enter the palace of our most illustrious queen."

The man led them through the double doors that were opened by posted guards. Once inside, the Iron Shore looked much like the any other seat of power he'd visited. The palace was richly appointed with a variety of materials and colors. The ceiling of the entryway rose upward through the core of the building to a height that would make him dizzy to scrutinize. Layers of wooden railings marking the perimeters of many floors were visible, but this form of architecture was familiar to him. It didn't have the same disorienting effect that the sparkling white city did. He noted, too, that there was a heavy presence of guards dotted around in ramrod stillness. Whether that was only because of the two foreign envoys or due to a constant fear of rebellion among Amira's own people was impossible to say at the moment. He would find out, however. A trade agreement was less valuable if the government was unstable, and diplomacy inclined to change with each new ruler.

A tall, thin woman dressed in a light blue gown that reminded him of winter ice approached. Because her head was completely uncovered, unlike the others they'd encountered, Ben could easily confirm for the first time that all the Iron Shore people tended to have white hair in mimicry of the stone around them. In Moorcondia, this was common for the aged. Here it was what marked these people as being different from the others who visited them — such as he and his bride. Even Kexen's flaxen hair looked dark in comparison. When the woman stopped in front of him, he could see that her eyes were the same shade as her dress.

The Master Prime Minister made the introductions. "Lord and Lady Tentrees, may I present Madam Chamberlain. She runs the operations of the palace for our queen and will show you to your suite. If you need anything, she will gladly accommodate your wishes."

The woman bowed her head. "It will be my honor. Please follow me."

Ben and Kexen did as asked, but when Ben scrutinized the staircase, he once more picked up his bride. He knew from experience that they'd likely being going up at least two more levels before reaching the one where guests were housed. This time, Kexen held on without objection. Ben could feel his bride's strength flagging, so he increased his pace, nipping at Madam Chamberlain's heels enough to silently demand that she do the same. On the fourth floor, she turned down the hallway to the right. Fortunately, she stopped at the first door they came across and opened it wide for them to pass. Ben entered a sitting room, only somewhat surprised to find that Baldrick and Euphemia were already there, carting pieces of luggage through the only doorway at the other end. Servants always had a way to make haste and beat their masters to their destination.

He put Kexen on his feet once more, keeping hold to steady him. "Thank you, Madam Chamberlain. My wife and I appreciate the lovely apartment your good queen has provided for us."

The woman's expression softened somewhat at the compliment. "You are Her Majesty's most welcome guest, Lord Tentrees. Anything I can do to make your visit with us more comfortable, please let me or one of my staff know." She paused. "May I assume that your wife will not be joining the banquet this evening?"

"Yes. The voyage was a rough one. My wife needs some food and rest, that is all."

"Of course. Shall I send the apothecary?"

Euphemia appeared abruptly to answer. "Many thanks, madam, but there is no need. I shall see to my mistress."

Madam Chamberlain stiffened and looked at Ben. He was quick to smooth things over. "Indeed, thank you, Madam. My wife's maid is well equipped to handle this unfortunate bout of seasickness."

"As you wish, my lord." With another bow of her head, the woman sailed out of the room, shutting the door behind her.

When they were alone, Euphemia was blunt. "I don't trust anyone here as far as I can throw them, which I can assure you is quite far indeed."

Ben couldn't argue with the woman's logic, and given that Kexen was sagging by the second, he prioritized settling his wife in. "Where is Lady Tentrees' bedroom?"

"There's only the one," Euphemia replied, gesturing to the inside doorway.

Ben helped Kexen through and over to the large canopy bed that dominated the room. He sat the boy on its edge, and once he was sure he was stable sitting without help, he stepped aside to give Euphemia room to undress her lady. What little energy Kexen had was clearly depleted. He let his maid manage him as if he were a rag doll. When the tall, strong woman had him in a thick nightgown, she tucked him into bed. Ben felt superfluous and a bit disappointed that his services were not needed. He wanted to continue to pamper and care for his wife — which was inappropriate. His time was better spent on planning the details of his diplomatic mission, given the new information he'd gathered with their arrival. No nuance was too small for him to incorporate into his strategy. Still, he hovered nearby, pleased when Kexen was able to at least drink the cup of water that Euphemia held to his lips.

"We should try some broth next," he said.

The maid gave him a banked look that nevertheless managed to convey that he was both speaking the obvious and interfering with her job. "I have already made that request, my lord."

Baldrick appeared from another doorway. "This way leads to the garderobe, my lord, and contains a closet sufficient to hold Lady Tentrees garments as well as yours. There is no separate space for you, and Euphemia and I are quartered on one of the servants' floor above." The man practically quivered with disapproval.

Ben clasped his hands behind his back. "Yes, well, we shall have to make do." Eyeing the bed he would have to share every night by necessity with his wife, he couldn't help but be grateful that the Iron Shore customs about housing a married couple would work in his favor. Sleeping by his side, Kexen would be perfectly positioned for Ben's intention to woo his wife and claim him in the manner he should have done from the beginning.

Chapter Five

"Benedict, Lord Tentrees, special envoy for the kingdom of Moorcondia."

Ben took in one more deep breath to settle his nerves before entering the throne room. He was relieved to see that it was like any other he'd seen, with courtiers dressed in their finest lining the carpeted path that led right to the platform where the queen of the Iron Shore sat. He kept his pace measured and took the time to study Queen Amira as courteously as his training permitted.

The small woman looked even younger than her official age, a function perhaps of her physical size, paleness and elaborate hair and clothing style. She reminded him of his sister's favorite porcelain doll. Her appearance suggested that someone had dressed her to play the part of a queen, the same way a toymaker might create an array of dolls to mimic various people—milkmaid, brewer, lady of the court. In this case, someone had seemed to decide that this is what a queen should look like. Although she wasn't that much different than Moorcondia's royal ladies, she somehow didn't look natural and appeared to be every bit as prone to cracking as his sister's doll had been when not treated carefully. Now, his lack of sleep was really taking its toll if he was lambasting himself over his childhood mistake.

Putting aside his thoughts, Ben concentrated instead on making a good impression. "Your Majesty. On behalf of King Auden of Moorcondia, I bring you greetings and thanks for your hospitality." He bowed low. When he straightened once more, he was startled to see the queen undergo a transformation.

Her face had broken into a wide smile. "Oh, Lord Tentrees, I'm ever so glad to have you visiting me for the whole winter. We are going to have such fun!" It was as if his sister's doll had suddenly come to life. It was disconcerting, to say the least.

The queen waved with her right hand, causing two men to step forward. "This is my betrothed, Prince Rupert. Isn't he a gorgeous man? And so amusing. We're all going to be spending a lot of time together."

The young man in question was a dandy unlike any Ben had ever seen. His attire rivaled that of the queen's. And this was new information. Ben hadn't known that the queen had officially taken her cousin as her fiancé, as had been intended by her late father. He'd been under the impression that she was enjoying her freedom. It was something of a relief, though. Perhaps it meant that there would be no overtures now from the queen to become intimate. Then again, the heat he saw in the man's eyes as he inclined his head in Ben's direction created a new worry.

"And this is Envoy Magnus from Far Isle. He arrived a few days ahead of you. But I expect you already know this," she added with a sly grin. "Such naughty boys you are, making us greet you ahead of schedule."

The Far Isle man's face betrayed nothing of his thoughts. His greeting was perfunctory and his manner of dress sober. It was, however, interesting to meet someone from that distant land in person for the first time. There had long been supposition that the people who'd colonized Far Isle had come from the Iron Shore, making the two people kindred countries. The idea had made sense, given the Iron Shore had limited space for its population to grow. Spreading out to distant lands seemed logical. Seeing the white hair and pale skin of the man, Ben could well believe the rumor. Unlike himself, Magnus could blend in as an Iron Shore man with no effort at all. His heart sank a little with the knowledge, but it also stiffened his resolve. He would make the treaty for Moorcondia, regardless.

The queen clapped her hands. "Now that we all know each other, we can go eat." She bounced out of her throne chair, and Ben thought it was some unknown physical law that permitted her to stand upright under what looked like heavy layers of clothing. Her gown was so stiff and elaborate that it almost appeared to have a life of its own. "Oh, but we will not have the pleasure of meeting your wife tonight, will we, Lord Tentrees?"

"Regrettably no, Your Majesty. The voyage was a difficult one. I'm sure Lady Tentrees will be recovered enough to meet you tomorrow evening…if you wish it."

"I certainly do! I'm dying to see Moorcondian fashions, and I hear your lady wife is particularly exotic, even among your own people."

Ben looked for censure in either tone or expression and found none. The Iron Shore queen appeared to be genuinely intrigued by Kexen. "Lady Tentrees is indeed unique, Your Majesty, if I may say so."

"Excellent," the queen gushed. "Come now, everyone. I'm famished." With that, the queen pranced down the three steps leading down from her throne and headed to her left.

The courtiers parted at her approach with heads bowed. The young woman moved with such grace that it looked as if she floated. Her head was held high and her expression serene and confident. However young this new queen was, he would do well not to underestimate her power or her intelligence.

* * * *

Kexen meandered through the paved paths of the royal garden, enjoying the invigorating cold air and the peace of solitude. No one else was out there, which he appreciated, needing time to acclimate to his surroundings now that he wasn't incapacitated by his seasickness. It was remarkable, actually, that an illness could vanish after a good night's sleep and by keeping food down. He didn't feel quite like his old self, but he was getting there, and he was determined to make his presentation to the Iron Shore queen that night. He felt guilty about having let Ben down in that regard, not that his husband had even hinted at disappointment. Quite the contrary, Ben had been marvelous throughout their journey, tending to him personally. Lingering anger over their wedding night had vanished in the face of his dire need for help and Ben's sure hand in giving it.

The man still hadn't pressured him, either, about wifely duties in bed. Kexen had woken when Ben had returned from the banquet and had known some anxiety that he would want to pick up where their wedding night had abruptly ended. But no, Ben had merely kissed his forehead after slipping under the sheets, wearing a nightshirt, before bidding him to go back to sleep. Then Ben had turned on his side away from him and promptly fallen asleep himself. It had taken Kexen a while longer to join him, and he'd felt rather peeved at the lack of interest. It was ridiculous, really, to worry about having sex and not having it at the same time. The conflicting feelings had continued to plague him when he'd woken late in the morning alone. Ben was busy with whatever meetings diplomats held all day, so after a simple breakfast, Kexen had decided to get some fresh air.

The wind stirred, sending a blast of cold up his skirts. He hadn't considered this inconvenient part of wearing women's clothing. He would see about securing thicker hosiery from Euphemia. The woman really was a marvel—quietly competent, always anticipating his needs. He was lucky to have her. That thought led him to ponder how the duchess was doing without him. Well, in all likelihood. Henry was a bright and eager lad. Kexen needed to accept the fact that he was never going to serve someone else again...unless one counted his husband. He'd been certain that was one thing he'd gladly provide. Now, he wasn't so sure. But he would tackle the problem as he'd always done any others—with optimism and determination. He would come to enjoy being mounted by his husband. The alternative didn't bear thinking of.

Kexen clasped his gloved hands in front of him to ward off the chill as he headed for a secluded corner tucked next to one of the palace's wings. He'd opted for a simple rose-colored gown with a matching peplum jacket trimmed with white fur. A headband of the same materials covered his ears. His soft, leather boots allowed him to walk almost silently. It had been marvelous fun picking out his new wardrobe with Mistress Camila. From what he'd seen, at least he could hold his own against the noblewomen of the court in this foreign land. The wind picked up, slapping against his cheeks, which was all to the good. The sickness had left him pale in an unattractive way. The cold might add some color so that he could go lightly on the face paint.

Something catching the waning sunlight in the near distance caught his eye. As he drew closer, he saw that it was a long hut made entirely out of glass. Inside it housed all kinds of greenery in sharp contrast to the winterized garden. He approached to get a better look. He'd never seen the like, and curiosity was one of his strengths or flaws, depending on how one looked at it. Some of the plants were familiar to him...others not. He walked down the length of the building to take it all in.

"May I help you?" Startled, Kexen whirled around. A middle-aged woman with black hair and copper skin stared at him with a not-unfriendly expression. Then she smiled. "Lady Tentrees, I presume?"

Not sure of the woman's station, Kexen gave a shallow curtsey. "I am, Madam. You have me at a disadvantage."

The woman's face became even more animated, and that was when Kexen noticed that there was something about her... "I am Madam Apothecary — Minna to my friends — and I do hope we will become just that."

Kexen grinned. "I think you are the first person I've met on the Iron Shore who has a first name."

Minna chuckled. "Oh, my dear Lady Tentrees, we all have one. It's just that the custom here is to recognize one's station or profession. Only royalty and nobility are referred to by their first names."

"Well, if it's not too bold, Madam, I prefer to be called Kexen."

"Then Kexen you shall be. I must say that I admire your bold choice in keeping your given name."

Confused, Kexen cocked his head. "I'm not sure I understand. What name should I use?"

Minna simply waved him forward. "Come. Let's go inside, share some tea and we can talk about that."

Kexen hesitated only a second before accepting the offer. Here could be his first real chance to help Ben. This apothecary surely knew much about the workings of the court and was clearly something of an outsider, as well. Her insights could prove invaluable. Besides, he worried it would be a lonely winter if all he had for company were his busy husband and their servants.

"May I ask what that glass house is?" They entered a wide wooden door into a cozy cottage attached to the palace.

"That is my greenhouse. I need to grow my medicinal plants year-round to supply the palace with the necessary drugs. It makes that possible during winter because I can regulate its temperature while still giving the plants the sunlight they need to flourish."

"It's extraordinary." Kexen pulled off his gloves and headband before unbuttoning his jacket.

A girl appeared from the far doorway. Minna motioned toward her. "Please take Lady Tentrees items and fix us a tea. Use my restorative herbs."

"Yes, ma'am." The cheery girl smiled shyly as she relieved Kexen of his outer clothing. Having been a servant himself, he could see that Minna was a kind mistress, given her maid's demeanor. That helped him relax as he followed his hostess into a parlor room that was warm from a blazing fire in the hearth.

Minna took a wing-backed chair in front of the fireplace and bade Kexen to take the other one. "I must compliment you on your ensemble, Kexen. You will cut quite the figure in court."

"You are too kind." The woman was dressed in a simple dark brown dress, so her opinion might not be as reliable as he would have liked.

As if sensing his thoughts, Minna smoothed her skirts. "Don't let my work gown fool you. When my dear husband was alive, I dazzled the old king's court somewhat myself. And I'm talking about Queen Amira's grandfather, by the way. That's how long I've been here, long enough to live under the rule of three people. The old king had a long reign, but Almira's father was taken from us far too early," she added in a soft voice.

"I'm sorry for your loss on both counts. Our last king was similarly struck down before his time."

Minna nodded. "The avian flu, was it not? A terrible thing, I hear. We were fortunate to avoid it. Isolation can be a good thing sometimes."

The maid entered with a tea tray. She put it on the table between them, and Minna dismissed her, pouring the cups herself. "You must drink this, Kexen. It will invigorate you after your terrible sickness."

Eager to try anything that could speed his recovery, he took a sip and was surprised to find it tasty. "Oh, that's lovely. If it is meant to be medicine, I would never have known."

"Medicine does one no good if it's too vile to drink. I have my ways of making anything palatable. I offered to bring you some last evening, but your maid was emphatic that you were on the mend. She is fiercely protective of you."

That was good to hear and not unexpected. Euphemia had shown her mettle during the voyage, and one only had to see the way her brother looked at Ben to know the measure of the man's loyalty. He and Ben couldn't ask for a better domestic couple to serve them. Kexen drank some more. "I suppose everyone knows about my unpleasant journey."

"Certainly. Everyone knows everything worth knowing on the Iron Shore. This diplomatic contest set up by the queen is all anyone has talked about since she announced it. Winter is going to prove to be most entertaining."

Kexen stared into his cup. "This mission is critical to my people, and I assume it's as much so for the Far Isle."

"I'm sure it is, my dear, and I am not one to criticize our queen, but I'm not going to defend her choice in her decision or how she chooses to handle it." She gave him a sly smile. "I think you'll find that your husband is the favored winner. That's certainly the gossip now that we can see both envoys."

"I am gratified to hear it, although I haven't met the Far Isle envoy myself yet."

"Prepare to be unimpressed." Minna sipped her own tea. "So, your name... If I may be so bold, I am curious as to why you chose to keep it, even though it says nothing of who you truly are. I apologize for my bluntness, but you are the first obvious kindred spirit of my acquaintance."

Kexen studied his hostess, her strong jaw and large hands making full understanding coming to him. "I have always been fortunate in being able to be true to myself my whole life. I love my name because my parents gave it to me. And where I came from, it is used for boys and girls alike. I can't imagine using another, in any event. And I am a complicated person — perhaps more than you are and blessed that my family accepted that about me. I have had the freedom to dress as I like and enjoy all manner of garb and styles. I typically choose my ensemble for the day, based on what pleases me in the moment. For now, because my husband asked it of me, I wear only women's clothing."

He drank more tea before continuing. "I have worried that Queen Amira and her court might not accept my marriage or me, for that matter, regardless of my mode of dress. Seeing you here in this important position, I can hope my worries are unfounded?" He raised his eyebrows, hoping for an answer.

Minna gave him a reassuring look. "They are. No one would dare disrespect you, and Queen Amira truly doesn't care. She's a bit wild in many ways."

"May I ask how you came to live here? Frankly, you look nothing like the other people of the Iron Shore."

"I *do* stand out, and certainly, I'm always happy to tell the tale of my life's journey. I am from a place not very far from here and more like I expect your own country to be. We farm, simply put, and export our excess harvest. It is a beautiful and peaceful land.

"I knew from the moment that I was able to form thoughts in my head that I was a girl. It was so obvious to me. I couldn't understand why my family kept acting as if I were a boy, although as I grew older, I understood that the fault lay with my body. It was wrong somehow, giving the appearance that I was something I was not. I tried to be understanding of my family, expecting that they would eventually come to see me as I truly was. I took to wearing one of my sister's old dresses when I could, when no one was watching me."

The woman's face took on an expression of wonder. "The first time I put it on, I felt truly *right*. It was a transformative experience, a complete vindication of what I knew to be my real self." Her face grew somber. "Then one day, my father found me doing so and beat me bloody for it. That's when I knew I had to keep my thoughts to myself. Even those I thought loved me were determined to continue the charade of my nature, no matter what. It was a dark day for me."

"I'm sorry."

"Thank you, but it's an old wound, my dear. And I have lived my life as I'd been born to for far more years, thanks to my darling husband. Vancel was the Master Apothecary here. He traveled all over the known world in search of medicinals to bring back, and one day that included coming to my own country. He was far older than I, but the moment he saw me, he actually *saw* me, the real one. It didn't matter what I wore, how I styled my hair or what I was called. His gaze went through all of that and struck my core. We fell in love just like that, and when he left, he took me with him."

"That must have been terrifying, regardless, running from the only home you'd ever known."

A look of sadness crossed the woman's face. "There was no fleeing involved. My father gladly accepted the coin Vancel offered."

"Oh, I see." Kexen felt that cut as if it had been inflicted on him. Not that he had any reason for complaint, but his marriage was not dissimilar to Minna's. Money had driven both of their fates. "My marriage was part of a trade deal between my family and Ben's."

"I can't say I'm surprised. Such unions are the norm all over the world. And I don't tell you this for sympathy, either, Kexen. My story has a happy ending, starting with that very night when Vancel claimed me as his own and told me I should pick a new name—one that was true to my nature. So I did. And by the time we'd arrived here, my transformation was complete. We shared a wonderful life together. He taught me his trade, and with his passing, I become the royal apothecary."

"I'm glad for you, Minna…and myself, if I may say so. I hope we will become fast friends."

"As do I. And if we are friends, may I ask if you like being married to a man?"

"I do, yes. Or rather I do in theory. The practical application of it has proven trickier than I thought. Some things don't fit quite as well as I'd imagined."

Minna chuckled. "My dear, I think I understand. And I have a few things that might make your introduction to married life easier…for both of you."

Kexen felt his cheeks heat. "We have oil."

"That's fine if you have nothing else—but not optimal. I have potions that loosen the inhibitions and salves that both ease the way and heat the blood. Never fear, Kexen. We will smooth the path of your marriage." She raised her eyebrows suggestively, and for the first time in many days, Kexen felt a weight being lifted from him.

* * * *

"I had no idea there would be dancing after supper." Kexen sat back in his chair, watching a few dozen couples prancing about the banquet room in elaborate and vigorous fashion. The bubbly queen was right in the middle, enjoying her Far Isle partner.

Ben leaned over to speak to him. His presence was a balm to Kexen's nerves. Minna's tea had bolstered his energy, but as the hour approached to be presented to the foreign queen, he'd become more worried that he wasn't up the task of representing his country. Confidence had always been something he'd had in abundance. It was disconcerting to realize that had only been true so long as he'd remained entrenched in the station to which he'd been born. Now that he was counted as nobility by reason of his marriage, he was no longer sure of himself. Fortunately, Ben had proven why he was such a good diplomat. He'd discerned Kexen's insecurity and had given him the emotional and physical support he'd needed. If not for the man's tight grip on his hand, Kexen might have toppled over making his curtsy to the queen.

"It was like this last evening as well. The queen loves this particular dance and so everyone performs it over and over with different music being played."

"Does that mean you're going to have to take a turn with her to keep up with the Far Isle envoy?"

"It would seem so. She partnered exclusively with her betrothed last night, but the level of the game has gone up."

"What will you do? We have nothing like this in Moorcondia." The last thing Kexen wanted was his husband's mission to be jeopardized by something as silly as a dance. He inwardly frowned at how the young queen was toying with people's lives.

"Not to worry, darling. I have watched the others and believe I can make a passible effort." Ben draped his arm around Kexen's shoulders, the gesture seemingly done without artifice.

The casual contact was nice. It made him feel as if their marriage was real in a simple way that had eluded them so far — not that there was more for him to feel of his husband at the moment other than the weight of his arm. Kexen's green and blue brocade gown was heavy material, and he'd styled it with a square neckline and stiff collar that skimmed the nape of his neck. He and Mistress Camila had reasoned that everyone's eyes would be drawn to the throat, thereby missing his lack of bosom. Ben had sweetly helped with the look by presenting him with a three-strand pearl necklace. It sat coolly on his breastbone, the perfect foil for the gown and his intent.

As the queen's small orchestra finished the music piece, the queen let go of Magnus' hands and faced the dais where the important diners sat, Kexen and Ben among them. Her gaze homed in on Ben, and she beckoned him with a little wave of her fingers. The look on her face irritated Kexen. Her obvious desire for his husband caused an unexpected spurt of jealousy. *Hussy!* Oh dear, where had that come from? He'd always believed in a freer sexual society, never one for conforming if he could get away with a little rebellion without too bad consequences. And he'd never given a second thought to the dalliances of married couples in the court. Everyone seemed happy with seeking pleasure with others. Why was it suddenly so different now that he had a husband who was being openly flirted with?

Maybe it's because, the law notwithstanding, it doesn't feel as if our marriage has been sealed into a permanent relationship.

He said nothing, of course, as Ben rose to join the queen, understanding the game they had to play, even as his resentment for it grew. Instead, he plastered a smile on his face and picked once more at the food in front of him. Minna had cautioned about eating too much and to stick with the blandest of what the meal had to offer. No alcohol, either — only water and fruit juice. He'd adhered to her advice, but at the moment, the glass of red wine sitting untouched before him had appeal.

"Lady Tentrees."

Kexen looked up to find Prince Rupert standing beside Ben's newly vacated chair. He dipped his gaze. "Your Highness."

A hand hovered before him. "Will you join me in the dance?"

Oh dear, he hadn't anticipated this. He'd assumed his presence would be relatively unremarkable after the first view of him by the queen and her court. Kexen licked his lips. "You are too kind, sir, but I fear I have no knowledge of the steps involved. Your toes will surely suffer for it."

The prince chuckled. "I will take the risk. Besides, I am an excellent teacher." He leaned in uncomfortably close to add, "You are in good hands with me."

Kexen had no choice other than to accept the proffered hand and allow the prince to escort him to the dance floor. He didn't like the almost possessive way the man gripped his hands. There was nothing to be done about it, though, as the steps required that kind of contact and it was better than the intimacy of a waltz. Having always been a good dancer, he picked up the routine, and he hated to admit it, but the prince did an excellent job of leading him through it. There was quite a bit of twirling about, and the prince's arm snared him at one point across the waist to execute a particular flourish. It lingered too long when the movements changed again. Kexen was an old hand at fending off unwanted advances, so he wasn't overly concerned with the interlude. Ben was a different matter, however. As Kexen's partner led him around, they came close enough to the queen and Ben for the man's expression to show. He did not like what he was seeing at all.

Oh, he's jealous. That thought cheered him a lot. Not that he wanted a possessive man, but the fact that Ben cared made Kexen feel wanted. Given the terrible way their marriage had gone so far, it wasn't crazy to worry that the man had become indifferent to having a wife, if not outright regretting the decision to marry at all. Thus far, Kexen hadn't been anything other than a burden. He was resolved that the situation would improve that very night. He plastered a pleasant smile on his face and did his part in making the mission a success. If he were very careful, he could be enticing without leading the prince on. It hopefully would enhance Kexen's image in this Iron Shore palace and help Moorcondia's cause.

But the vast room was warm from all the many, energetic bodies. His sickness having weakened him, Kexen hadn't realized he was becoming dizzy until one final twirl by the prince had him stumbling and falling. He never hit the floor, however. Strong arms caught him into a sturdy embrace. He expected to see the prince holding him, but it was Ben. Kexen blinked up at him as his husband held him upright. If he'd thought there would be censure in that gaze, or embarrassment, he would have been wrong. Ben's expression clearly showed only worry.

"We have overtaxed you, darling. It's time for you to retire."

Kexen wasn't going to argue the point. Now that he had stopped moving, he could feel his strength draining. Still, it was early. "We mustn't leave before the queen." His protest was marred by his breathless quality.

"I've already made our excuses. I could see you fading with each turn. She understands," he added.

Kexen wasn't convinced. "If you leave now, Magnus will fill the void."

"The winter will be long, and there will be plenty of time to make my case for Moorcondia. For now, I'm getting you into bed." With that, he swept Kexen into his arms and carried him out.

Chapter Six

Ben slid his arms into the sleeves of his dressing gown that Baldrick held open. He'd adopted the habit of sleeping in his small clothes, instead of being nude, for the sake of his wife's sensibilities. He didn't want his needs to be unspoken demands beyond which Kexen was up to doing, physically or emotionally. The bit of cloth hugging his loins was a simple, yet effective barrier...unless one looked too closely. Try as he might, he couldn't quite get his erection to go down. He'd been ragingly hard since seeing Prince Rupert dancing with Kexen, too much interest being shown by the queen's fiancé than he would have liked. It was just as well that Kexen had succumbed to tiredness. If Ben had noticed the prince's interest in his wife, others of the court may have as well, and the queen was shrewd under all that makeup and girlish demeanor. The fact that she was flirting and possibly more with other men didn't mean she was okay with Rupert doing the same. The last thing the mission needed was *that* unforeseen drama.

It wasn't only jealousy or anger, however, that was causing his arousal. It was more the way his bride fit so perfectly in his arms, the allure of the boy's beautiful face and the fact that Ben hadn't been able to enjoy the benefits of marriage that kept him hard and wanting. He considered sleeping in the dressing gown, given that he was going to be slipping into bed at the same time as his wife. The previous night, he'd gone to bed after Kexen had fallen asleep, hoping the mattress was wide enough that he could lie without disturbing the boy. Although that hadn't happened, it had been easy to settle down with little interaction. This evening would be different, at least visually. If nothing else, the glow of the fire would highlight his aroused state. It wasn't that he was embarrassed to let his wife know how much he wanted him. It was more a matter of giving Kexen space. Through his own stupidity, Ben had set back their marital bond. It was up to him to rectify the situation with Kexen's needs in mind, and making him feel duty-bound would not be helpful.

That wasn't to say Ben intended to have an entirely chaste evening. His wife had wanted a bath to wash away the heat of the dance. Because Ben had taken to using the sitting room for his personal grooming, he hadn't been there to see Kexen being undressed and slipping into the warm water. But he could hear him — the soft murmurs of Kexen and Euphemia, the rustling of clothing coming off, the lapping within the tub. Their suite was simply too small to hide even low noises. The images forming in Ben's mind were driving him a little mad. He had to do something, even if it only benefited his wife in the immediate future. They needed to begin their marriage anew, and it was Ben's duty to see to it.

He belted his robe. "Thank you, Baldrick. That will be all for the evening." He jutted his chin at the doorway. "I'm going to release your sister for the night as well, so you should wait to escort her to her chamber."

"As you wish, my lord."

Ben flashed a smile. "I intend to play lady's maid for the rest of the evening."

With that, he entered first the bedroom, then the garderobe, which also contained a long, narrow stone tub. The Iron Shore had excellent plumbing, so the steaming water had been easily called up with a twist of the faucet handle. Kexen lay reclined within, his head resting against a towel over the back slope. His hair was pinned up in a messy bun and his body was submerged up to his shoulders in water cloudy from some kind of soap. A pleasant scent Ben recognized as lavender permeated the room. He felt relaxed himself merely from setting foot inside it. His appearance, however, must have registered with his wife because Kexen's eyes flew open even before Euphemia could say anything.

"Ben, is something wrong?"

"Not at all, darling. Given the lateness of the hour, I wanted to let Euphemia seek her bed. I can take over for her here." He gave the woman a look that signaled she shouldn't argue the point. With a brief nod, she bid them both good night and left.

Kexen started to rise. "I'm done with my bath, anyway. I'll dry off and dress for bed."

Ben gestured with his hand for him to lie back down as he approached the tub. "No need to get up so soon. The water looks warm still, and I imagine you didn't have time to wash."

"It's not necessary. I merely wanted to rinse off before retiring." Kexen nevertheless complied with Ben's entreaty and settled back into place again.

Ben kneeled beside the tub and picked up a soft cloth and bowl of soap lying there on the floor. "It would seem Euphemia had a full wash in mind." He flashed a smile. "Let me do the honors."

Kexen looked slightly alarmed. "There is no need. I can do it myself." He reached for the items in Ben's hand.

Ben held them out of reach. "Nonsense. You would deny me the pleasure?"

Kexen's eyes narrowed as he sank back down. "I must lack imagination, because I've done this job many times myself for the Duchess of Vostguard, and while hardly difficult, I can't say I enjoyed it."

Ben chuckled as he dipped the cloth in the bowl and scooped soap into it. "I should hope not. Prince Soren wouldn't have liked his good wife's personal groomer coveting him in the bath."

"Huh! As if I ever would have. The duchess is a lovely person and a great beauty, but my tastes run in a different direction. And I'm not certain what fun can be had in a bath. A lake, yes," he added with a cock of his head. "On a warm summer night, stripping down and swimming with a friend can be quite delicious. This tub is far too narrow, however, for those types of antics."

Ben tamped down the spurt of jealousy that came from picturing his wife frolicking in water with some long-ago paramour. *He's mine now.* "That may be, but I am simply offering to clean your lovely skin."

So saying, Ben leaned over and ran the soapy cloth in slow circles on Kexen's chest before sliding it over to the nearest shoulder and down its arm. He was rewarded almost instantly with a soft sigh escaping Kexen's lips. "I want you to know that you made an excellent presentation to the queen this evening. You were beautiful yet did not upstage her, and your manners were impeccable. I think everyone was impressed, as well, that you'd rallied from your sickness to make the effort."

Kexen looked at him through narrowed eyes as Ben lifted the arm to wash it all the way round. "Thank you, but you seem surprised that I could pull it off."

Ben paused. Damnation, it hadn't been his intent to be condescending. "My apologies, darling. I didn't mean to imply that at all." He resumed the washing. "It was my clumsy attempt at reassuring you. I knew unreservedly when I asked for your hand that you would be an asset to my mission — to all of them, actually. This one happens to be particularly difficult."

Ben lowered Kexen's arm before starting back with the chest and repeating the process on Kexen's other side. Because he had to lean over his wife to do so, he easily detected the increasing speed of Kexen's breath. Ben smiled inwardly at delight over how well his plan was working. If nothing else, his wife was a very sexual being. All it took to coax that out was diligence and patience.

Kexen softly coughed once. "We haven't, um... discussed this mission very much." There was a restlessness to his body now. "Would the Iron Shore be a new source of iron for Moorcondia?"

Ben slid the cloth along the back of his wife's hand, studying the slender fingers and smoothly rounded nails. "No. We've been trading with his country for a long time...as has Far Isle. What's different is that now

Amira has decided to only supply one of us." Replacing the arm in the water, he returned to the torso, swirling the cloth down toward the abdomen, not caring that the submerged cloth wasn't holding any more soap. Cleaning wasn't really the purpose of his attention. "Her justification is that it will be cheaper for them to have only one trade route to maintain, but I'm not convinced that is true. The economics only support it somewhat. We supposed this might be a pretext for her to hold one big, long, exciting party. Having met her, I can well believe that to be the case."

Kexen quivered at the touch. "That is hardly the basis for good government. And if we lose to Far Isle, how will Moorcondia find a replacement source?" The boy's voice was becoming breathless.

"That is a good question, darling." Ben stopped his movement downward before reaching Kexen's groin. On a glance, a hardening cock could be seen through the cloudy water. He hid a grin of satisfaction while he wrung out the cloth and lathered it once more. He slid down the side of the tub to reach Kexen's legs. He cupped the back of one knee to raise the nearest one out of the water and applied his efforts to the thigh.

"Moorcondia has its own iron ore, as well as other sources outside of our borders. We will make do while reaching out even farther to discover other countries. It won't be catastrophic if we lose out to Far Isle, but it will put a strain on our supplies — and my career will undoubtedly suffer from the failure."

Because washing Kexen's shapely leg was more pleasurable than contemplating the consequences of his own possible defeat, Ben went silent and concentrated on his current task. Besides, he had deliberately not spoken to his bride in detail about what was at stake. He didn't want him to overly worry. The success of the mission lay squarely with himself and no one else.

Kexen was more than a pretty face with a passion for clothing, however. Even though Ben's efforts were having the hoped-for effect, Kexen's mind apparently wasn't being derailed from the topic. "Surely the king sent you because he has great confidence in your ability. And by that measure, would he really punish you if a capricious young queen chose Far Isle over Moorcondia? That hardly seems fair."

Ben laid the first leg back into the tub and picked up the other one. Because of the angle, he had no trouble seeing that his bride was now fully erect. It was a pleasing sign that he could do that for his wife and that he was feeling well enough to become aroused. "Rulers don't have to be fair, darling. Although, that said, our king is more so than others, I believe. Please don't fret over it. You need only continue to be yourself and enjoy our time here." Instead of lingering over Kexen's calf, he slid the cloth up the inner thigh to brush against the balls.

Kexen jerked on a moan, then said, "I want to help. I am not afraid of doing so."

Ben dropped both the cloth and the pretext of merely bathing his wife. He first cupped Kexen's balls, then his shaft. "I know you can do anything you set your mind to, my darling. But first you need rest, and I don't think that will happen unless I address this little problem." He squeezed lightly and flicked his thumb through the slit. "It's only fair that I do so, given that I believe I am the cause of it."

Kexen moaned again and bucked into Ben's grip. The boy's eyes were fully closed now and his lips were parted in a small O. His breath came out in staccato puffs. "Gods, Ben."

Ben began to jerk his wife with long, slow movements. He'd been with enough men to know that his wife wasn't going to last long. And as much as he wanted to draw out the experience for both their sakes, it was late, and his bride needed his sleep. So Ben brought him to a climax quickly, enjoying the way the orgasm played out over Kexen's face. The boy cried out as he arched his back. Ben moved to hold him steady to keep his head from sliding under the water. Because of the contact, he could feel every tremor that shook his bride's body. When Kexen finally went limp, Ben smiled broadly at the pleasure he'd brought to his wife, and the relief to himself that he hadn't completely ruined his marriage with his oafish behavior on their wedding night. He felt confident that with care and patience, he could repair the damage completely.

With the water growing cold and his knees protesting their time spent on the tile floor, Ben reluctantly stood and grabbed the large towel Euphemia had put out. Then he plucked Kexen from the tub and wrapped him tightly before carrying him into the bedroom and over to the fireplace. He sat down on one of the wing-backed chairs, settling Kexen on his lap with his head against his chest, and began to rub his bride dry.

On a sigh, Kexen said, "You really don't need to do this. I am not so drained from your ministrations that I can't take care of myself."

Ben chuckled. "My darling, you cut me to the quick. I pride myself on being able to render another senseless."

Kexen raised his head and pried open his eyes. "I trust I'm the only one you intend to try that with at this point."

The small show of jealousy delighted Ben. He pressed a kiss on Kexen's nose. "Yes indeed, darling. No need to worry about that."

It was wonderful simply sitting there with his wife, that pert rump of his pressing against Ben's own erection. But it was late, and he had an early morning meeting with the queen. He had no doubt it was the beginning of her really putting him through his paces, and he needed rest to be as sharp as possible — not to mention that in the next second Kexen stifled a yawn.

"Time for bed."

Ben rose before Kexen could offer an argument, if he'd even intended to. Ben slid the nightgown Euphemia had left on the bed over Kexen's head, let down his hair and tucked him in for the night. The boy looked both enticing and vulnerable lying there, nearly swallowed by the downy mattress and the thick comforter. It was quite the contrast, causing a brief war within Ben. The urge to continue sexual play was strong. Logic and compassion won out. His dick be damned, he was sticking with the original plan. He gave Kexen a quick kiss, straightening when the boy seemed to be reaching to keep him close.

"Good night, Kexen." He went to turn down the wall-mounted lamps. The room was left in the golden glow of the banked embers in the fireplace.

Ben went to his side of the bed and, shedding his dressing gown, slid in next to his wife. He intended to remain completely separate from the boy, but Kexen had other ideas. He rolled against Ben and placed his hand right on top of Ben's cramped erection.

"There is one thing left unattended." Kexen squeezed, forcing a groan out of Ben.

Oh, how tempted he was to take that hand and slip in under his small clothes. Like his wife had been, he was primed. It would take very little to set him off. But that wasn't part of the plan. If their marriage was to grow into something deeper with trust and affection, he needed to show Kexen that his needs were more important than Ben's.

Reluctantly, he lifted that hand and placed it on Kexen's own hip. "That is nothing for you to worry about. I am fine as I am. You must get some sleep."

There was a snort of disagreement. "But, Ben, that's ridiculous." Kexen tried to move his hand back.

Ben stopped him more firmly this time. "It will be as I say, darling. What I did for you was my pleasure without any expectation of a return other than your finding it enjoyable."

"And I did. Surely that was obvious."

"Indeed, most gratifying."

"Now it's time for me to return the favor." There was a pause. "I am your wife. It is my duty—"

Ben cut Kexen off by facing him and placing a finger on his lips. "There will be no talk of *that*. I am your husband, not your king. You owe me only as much affection as you wish to give." He rolled onto his back again. "Our courtship was too short and my expectations for both of us unfair. From this point forward, I intend to court you as you deserved to be. We have the whole winter, and by its end, I hope to have wooed you into my arms because it's where you want to be, not out of a sense of obligation."

"Really, that's not necessary." There was a tone of exasperation.

Ben decided to exercise his prerogative of being the master of the marriage to put an end to the conversation. "Go to sleep, Kexen. We will speak no more of this. Not tonight, anyway."

There was a moment of silence before Kexen rolled onto his side away from him. Ben could sense annoyance in his bride and hoped he hadn't undone what he'd accomplished in the bath. His bride was exhausted, regardless. It took no time before his breathing evened out. Ben lay there with his aching balls and straining dick, willing himself to join his wife in slumber. Relieving himself was out of the question. It would merely aggravate his wife more if he seemed to be choosing his own hand over the boy's touch. No, he needed to get his body under control by force of will only. The next day, his mission was going to start in earnest. He needed strength if he was going to succeed.

* * * *

"Ah, Lord Tentrees, do come and sit next to me."

Ben offered the queen a bright smile as he did as she commanded. On the way over to the long settee, he nodded cordially to Master Prime Minister, who sat opposite his queen in her personal study. It was surprisingly cozy, given its vast size. Ben was both grateful for the man's presence and annoyed by it. Being alone with the queen could give Ben a chance to make his case for Moorcondia without interruption, but it might also make her bolder. It still wasn't clear if she viewed Ben as fair game or not. Reminding himself that he had all winter to woo the queen, he concentrated on pleasing her while keeping his distance. Fortunately, the queen's voluminous velvet skirts forced him to sit outside of her arm's reach. He was lucky in making use of the natural barrier.

"Good morning, Your Majesty. It's a beautiful day."

The queen giggled in a girly way. "Did you see that it snowed overnight? It always makes the palace sparkle."

"I did, yes. And the white stone is a perfect foil, enhancing your already magnificent home." The first rule of diplomacy was to find truths, however small, and shower your host with them.

"Yes, I'm very fortunate in my station in life." The girl's expression turned into sadness in the blink of an eye. "This will be my first winter since my dear papa died. It will be bittersweet, but I must put on a brave face, no matter what. Isn't that right, Master Prime Minister?"

The man schooled his features into one that conveyed both sympathy and reassurance. "Yes, Your Majesty. We all feel the loss of our king, who was taken from us so unexpectedly, no matter how grateful we are to have you as our esteemed ruler."

Amira preened obviously at the blatant compliment. "I find comfort in that and also that he at least died doing something he loved." She turned to Ben. "You do know the story of his fate?"

Like everyone else in Moorcondia, he only knew what the Iron Shore was careful to release into the world. "A hunting accident, was it not?"

The queen looked at her bejeweled hands sitting on her lap. "Yes. Wild boar. They're so dangerous, but Papa loved riding after them and skewering them with a spear."

Ben thought that the old king had been very stupid indeed. Dangerous animals like that should have been hunted from afar with crossbows. He supposed monarchs felt invincible unless they saw one of their own cut down in front of them. He knew Auden had been humbled by his parents' death. Perhaps Amira was the same. "A tragedy to be sure, Your Majesty, but he sounds like a brave man."

"Yes, he was! It was his horse that failed him. It stumbled and crushed him. Stupid thing," she added with a grimace. "It had to be put down, of course. Master Prime Minister was with him and can tell the tale better than I." She looked at the man expectantly.

"Yes, I was," the man said gravely. "It was a horror to witness, but there is some comfort in knowing he didn't suffer."

The king or the horse? Ben kept that insolent query to himself, naturally. "There is a blessing in that."

The mercurial queen went from profound sadness to excited joy in the next moment. "Well, I'm the queen now, and I'd love to show you around my palace, Lord Tentrees."

"I am honored, Your Majesty." He stood immediately and bowed. This was a chance for him to start his diplomatic wooing.

The queen got to her dainty feet, shaking out her skirts. "We'll start with my favorite part." She glanced at the now-standing Master Prime Minister. "You may return to your office. I wish to be with Lord Tentrees alone."

The man clearly didn't like that, but he banked his feelings very quickly. "As you wish, Your Majesty." He shot what Ben considered to be a warning look as he left.

That seemed pointless. What did he think Ben was going to do in his absence? It would be suicidal to do anything to hurt the girl, and this entire game was one of her making. Surely she set the rules and everyone else simply went along with them. And in the end, 'alone' turned out to be a matter of interpretation. As he walked one step behind Amira, they were followed by two ladies in waiting and a plethora of guards. That was in addition to the sentries who were stationed along the way. Ben was careful to keep his hands clasped behind his back, lest someone misinterpret any of his movements.

The queen kept up a steady stream of nonsense that Ben nevertheless listened keenly to. Sometimes important information could be gleaned in such chatter. She led him into the back of the palace, the corridors becoming narrower with walls and floors of ancient stone far different than the ornate materials of the newer part of the building. This was undoubtedly the original seat of power for the Iron Shore, the part from which the rest of it had grown over the many generations of rulers. With each step, Ben could see how previous monarchs had added to the structure. It surprised him that the queen came to this part of her home, let alone wanted to show it to anyone. There was nothing pretty about it and it had to remind her of how her lofty station had more humble origins. At the end of the final hallway, they came to wooden double doors with heavy black iron fixtures. Two guards flanked them. They stiffened at their queen's arrival before opening them on a silent command.

"This is where it all started," Amira intoned before sailing into a dark room that was lightened only by the sun that streamed through stained-glass windows on either side. At the far end stood an ornately carved wooden throne. Amira walked down an aisle flanked by sturdy benches to hop upon the chair. As short as she was, her feet dangled over it inches from the floor. That fact didn't take way from the powerful presence she conveyed. When she looked at Ben and beckoned him with a wave of her hand, he could feel the weight of the power that she held. It was a humbling and fascinating feeling. Moorcondia's royal family was as old as this one, but there was nothing left of the original palace as far was he was aware. He hadn't appreciated how much obvious history could enhance the claim to govern a country.

He stopped in front of the throne and stared at the intricate design that marked Amira's literal seat of power. The pattern was unlike any he'd ever seen before, stylistic and showing no images of what lived in the natural world. Every other ancient throne he'd seen and many of the new ones portrayed animals that were used as symbols for the royal house. These carvings appeared to convey only beauty. "It is magnificent." There was no need for a studied tone in stating this clear truth.

Amira rubbed her fingers along the arm of her chair. "This is where my ancestors of untold generations have been anointed by the priests. I, myself, was here mere months ago after my father died. The ceremony held in my current throne room for all the court to see was mere pageantry. What happened in this sacred room was conveyed by the hands of the gods."

Ben kept his expression neutral. He was at best a half believer in the existence of the gods and what role they played in people's fates, if any. Regardless, he could understand how anyone seeing this place, standing in it bathed by its eerie, yet beautiful colored light would feel the presence of a force beyond their understanding.

No wonder Amira acted with such confidence, even as young as she was. If he had been put through a ceremony surrounded by such grave imagery, he would have felt entitled to do anything he wanted to, too.

"I am in awe, Your Majesty."

"As you should be." The girlish tone was gone, replaced by a more mature-sounding woman. "I was and still am. It was during my anointment that I finally felt the full weight of my destiny. I will do what's best of the Iron Shore, and that includes establishing the most beneficial trade agreements for it."

"Of course, ma'am."

She studied her fingers where she continued to caress the throne's arm. "I begged my father to hold off on the formal engagement to Rupert. I wanted more time to enjoy myself. Once I was queen, I realized that I need to reassure my people that my line will continue, so I made the engagement a formal one—not that I intend to marry too quickly. I deserve the fun of freedom for a while longer." She smiled suggestively.

Sensing a danger, Ben resisted the temptation to step back from the girl. It was silly, really, to be concerned. It wasn't as if the queen was going to pin him to the ancient stone floor and ride him in front of all those peering eyes behind him. *Would she?* No, her very words confirmed her reverence for their location. He also knew how to deflect the innuendo.

"I understand the desire, Your Majesty. I took my time before marrying as well, although I can report that it is a state that has made me very happy." He smiled broadly and hopefully harmlessly.

The queen frowned briefly before saying, "Hmm-m, your wife is quite lovely. Unusual, as well, although I gather you like that about Lady Tentrees."

Definitely more clever than she looks. He would do well to keep that in mind. "Yes, I do, ma'am. We are well-matched as a married couple."

"I'm sure. Rupert and I are, too — at least, one would think so. We are related after all and grew up together." She sighed. "I suppose it's best for my people to see that connection, even though many of my station are wed as part of diplomacy with other countries. Was it your intention to convince me to marry a Moorcondian prince?"

The direct and unexpected question threw him for a moment before he answered. "It wasn't, Your Majesty. Although my king didn't know that you had formalized your engagement with Prince Rupert, he had known of your father's intent. And while he has a second son who is destined to be matched in way that benefits Moorcondia, I was not tasked with singing the boy's praises to you." Ben hoped the queen wouldn't encourage him to do so. Even *his* diplomatic skills would be taxed trying to paint the profligate boy in positive terms.

"Good! It would be boring, to say the least." The queen jumped off her throne. "Let's go to my jewel room. It's my second favorite place in the palace. I have so many pretty things to wear."

And just like that, the spell of the area was broken. Ben stood to one side as Amira passed, then followed in her wake, happy to be heading back somewhere he understood better. Plus, he liked looking at jewelry himself. Nothing said he couldn't enjoy his mission in order to accomplish it.

Chapter Seven

"Are the people in the Iron Shore always so...reserved?" Despite feeling quite comfortable in Minna's presence, Kexen didn't want to say anything offensive about the woman's adopted country. It was strange, though, to wander through the open market without anyone staring at him. It was as if he were no more remarkable than any other person there, except he was the unusual wife of a foreign diplomat. Moorcondians would have shown far more curiosity.

"It is their way, yes," Minna replied as she weaved through the stalls of wares. "Outside of winter, ships come from all over to trade with us. They are used to strangers and take it as a point of pride that they treat everyone with equal privacy and would consider it rude to show more interest."

Minna came closer to link her arm with Kexen's and added in a quieter voice, "I can assure you they are fascinated by your presence and are eager for you to buy their goods."

Kexen was content with the leisurely stroll through the city center with his new friend. Minna was easy to talk to and a font of knowledge. It was good to get out of the small suite that he shared with Ben, while not having to engage in stilted conversation with other members of the court. The walk in the brisk morning air also gave him time to mull over the previous evening's unexpected end and how he felt about Ben's stated strategy for their marriage. His gentle ministrations in the bath had left Kexen still feeling relaxed, but his refusal to do more or allow Kexen to return the favor was vexing. This all seemed to stem from guilt, and while Kexen remained irked over their wedding night, he trusted Ben and wanted to get on with the pleasure of marriage. With the help Minna had given, he was confident that he could come to enjoy his husband's intimate invasion.

Because thinking about it aroused him in an untimely fashion, Kexen put aside those thoughts and concentrated on perusing the merchants' wares. A stall containing carved bowls of various sizes and shapes in a dark wood he'd never seen before caught his attention. "What's this?" He gently tugged his companion in that direction.

"These are from Far Isle," Minna said. She let go of Kexen's arm. "Feel free to examine anything you like. The merchant will not mind."

Kexen took Minna at her word, and after a brief nod of acknowledgment to the woman standing behind the counter, he leaned down to peer at the bowls more carefully. One in particular caught his eye. He lifted it carefully to study its design. "How lovely."

Minna stood beside him. "It's a trinket bowl. Many ladies keep favorite pieces of jewelry in them in particular. They fit easily on a vanity, making them readily available after bathing."

Kexen held the item up to the light. The design was unlike any he'd ever seen before, a delicate yet intricate pattern. "I can see that it's one of those things that's simply pretty to have, even if a practical use cannot be manufactured."

Minna chuckled. "I suppose so. One of the benefits of having money, I have found, is the ability to indulge oneself now and again. You should buy it."

Kexen's instinctive reaction was that it was likely too costly, then he remembered that he had money now. After that, he also remembered that he had none of the gold coins that everyone accepted as currency on him. He put the bowl back on the counter. "Alas, I didn't bring my reticule."

Minna rolled her eyes. "My dear, you simply take it, and the merchant will send the chit to the palace for your husband to pay."

Kexen glanced at the merchant, who nodded solemnly in agreement. "Oh." That made everything easier, and it was something he found he really wanted. His new station and wealth meant he should accept indulging himself more than he was used to—not that he expected Ben to buy bobbles for him. He could handle the payment himself once the bill arrived. "How much do you want?" The merchant named a sum that seemed reasonable to Kexen, but Minna intervened before he could agree to it.

"Oh dear, I do apologize, Lady Tentrees. I had no idea it would be priced so high. It's only a *wooden* bowl, not one made of gold." Taking Kexen by the arm, she started to tug him away.

The merchant jumped to respond. "It may be wood, Madam Apothecary, but it's one that's only found in Far Isle. You won't see the likes of it anywhere else. And look at its carving. That is a pattern used only in Far Isle, as well, but rarely. Very few craftspeople are even permitted to. It no doubt took its maker an entire season to complete."

Minna shrugged. "I'm sure, but it's no reason to pick Lady Tentrees' pockets."

The merchant harrumphed. "Well, seeing as how the esteemed lady is a visitor to our great country, I suppose I can give a small discount."

"Only a small one?" Minna's lovely face took on the look of a warrior about to do battle. And that was when the real haggling began.

* * * *

Kexen returned to his suite with the bowl wrapped in soft cloth, buoyed by the shopping trip and spending time in Minna's company. They'd shared a cup of restorative tea before Kexen had left to have lunch, hopefully with his husband. He smiled broadly when he saw the man sitting at a table set with a delicious smelling meal and headed in that direction.

Euphemia ambushed him before he got far. "Let me take your things, my lady." Kexen surrendered his cloak, hat and gloves, but balked when his maid tried to take the bowl.

Instead, he unwrapped it and took it over to the table to show Ben. "Look what I bought." He held it up, even as his husband rose to give him a too quick and too chaste kiss on the cheek.

"How lovely. Such an unusual type of wood." He held Kexen's chair for him before returning to his own. "Where did you get it?"

Setting it to one side, Kexen waited until his plate has been placed before him by Baldrick before answering. "At the open-air market in the heart of the city. It's said to be from Far Isle and made out of wood only found there. Its design in particular caught my eye, so exotic, and according to the merchant, uncommon."

Ben peered at the bowl more closely. "It is, yes, although…the pattern is familiar somehow." He sat back again. "How did you get to that marketplace?"

"Minna took me."

Ben nodded at his manservant as he accepted his own meal. "Ah yes. The interesting Madam Apothecary. I'm glad that she has become such a fast friend, but remember that we must always be circumspect, no matter how comfortable we become with anyone here."

"I know." Kexen picked up his fork and started on the piece of grilled pink fish in front of him. While he understood his husband's concerns, he couldn't help believing that Minna was an ally, not someone trying to gain advantage or waiting for an opportunity to curry favor with the queen by telling tales about him or Ben. "She is a master at haggling price. I am quite pleased with the purchase. Which reminds me, as is the custom here, you will be sent a request for payment. Please hand it over to me to take care of."

Ben paused with his forkful of food halfway to his mouth. "My darling, I will do no such thing. It is my honor to shower you with whatever gifts you'd like."

Kexen was both pleased and irritated. He didn't want to worry about spending too much of Ben's money when he now had his own. "That's not necessary. I can afford —"

"I am aware of the prince's generous gift, *wife*. But I assure you that I receive a handsome wage from the crown and a hefty distribution from my family's business. We don't need your money."

Kexen saw the look on his husband's face and heard the tone of his voice. This was about pride — dumb, male pride. His instinctive reaction was to call him on it, then dismiss the nonsense and insist on paying for the bowl himself. Something stopped him. He wasn't the same boy who'd flitted about the Moorcondian palace, flirting with those men he liked and cutting those he didn't down to size. He was married now — a *lady*, no less. He had made the promise to live in Ben's world for the rest of his life. That meant submitting to the man's will. That was especially true when it cost him nothing. His sense of self-worth would not be diminished letting his husband treat him to a silly bowl.

Plastering a serene look on his face, Kexen said, "I understand, and thank you for the gift."

His easy acquiescence obviously pleased the man. "You're welcome, darling. How much was it, by the way?"

Kexen named the price and was immature enough to enjoy the way Ben swallowed hard on the news. They sat in silence for a while, eating their lunch. It was delicious. The Iron Shore had excellent food, especially that which came from the sea. It was going to be interesting to try each new dish put in front of him.

"Oh, by the way," Ben said as he wiped his mouth, "the queen has asked us to go ice skating with her and her entourage later this afternoon. The palace has a pond that freezes over, and they've erected rails to help people navigate the ice. I, for one, will be relying heavily on that and hope that I don't disgrace myself."

Kexen nearly clapped his hands with excitement. "Oh, how wonderful! I love ice skating."

"You've done it before?"

"Of course. It's a common pastime in the Outer Vale during the winter. Is it not also in Northcliff?"

Ben grimaced. "No. We have the South Sea on one side and a few small ponds dotted around. They freeze over, of course, but the most we do is ice fishing. Skating seems like a wasted effort. It's just going around in circles, after all."

"It's fun," Kexen retorted, surprised at how serious his husband's people seemed to be. "Not everything has to have a purpose, Ben."

"I suppose not." He drained his glass of wine, then stared at it thoughtfully. "Here and now, however, it does. The queen is far shrewder than she appears. We have to assume that every activity she expects us to join in on is part of her overall goal of pitting us against Far Isle. I am very grateful to you, darling, that you can meet the challenge, even if I cannot." He smiled at him warmly.

Heat flared in Kexen's belly. Memories of his evening bath surfaced unbidden, reminding him of how much pleasure could be found after all in their marriage. Desire made him bold. "If we have time, I would like to take a nap so that I am in fine form for the exercise."

"An excellent idea, darling. We mustn't forget how sick you were on the journey. It was only a few days ago."

"Yes, I feel fine but it's better to be cautious." Kexen licked his lips in a gesture that he knew drew a man's gaze there. "Would you like to take it with me?" A bold suggestion. Then again, he was in a bold mood. He really was back to his old self, apparently.

Ben dashed his hopes by waving away the suggestion. "No, I will only disturb your rest."

Disappointed yet still determined, Kexen rose and went over to his husband. Putting his hand on Ben's arm, he tried again. "Do you have urgent matters to attend to before the skating party?"

Ben's gaze went from the hand touching him to Kexen's face. There was a heat to his eyes, even as he said. "No, but..."

Kexen tugged. "Come. I will rest better with you beside me." He pursed his lips and fluttered his lashes.

Ben coughed once before rising and clasping Kexen's hand in his own. "If it will help you, then of course, I shall." He waved away the servants as he led Kexen to their bedroom. "You are dismissed until an hour before the queen's skating party begins. I will see to my lady wife myself," he added as they sailed through the doorway. He shut the door behind them to provide immediate privacy.

Then he whirled Kexen into his arms and kissed him with a hunger that he'd only shown before on their wedding night. At the time, it had been a new experience, because Ben had always been reserved, even in their most intimate moments prior to that. He seemed to be making up for his earlier reticence by devouring Kexen's mouth, while at the same time shedding him of his gown. The man's dexterity was impressive. The laces in the back came undone almost immediately, allowing Ben to slide the bodice past

Kexen's shoulders to pool around his waist. Ben maneuvered them over to the bed and lifted Kexen to sit on the edge. He stood between Kexen's splayed legs, sweeping his tongue around every corner of Kexen's mouth while roaming his hands over every inch he could reach. The feel of his slightly rough hands against Kexen's bare arms sent shivers through him. When Ben broke the kiss, Kexen gave a mewl of protest.

Ben chuckled as he knelt before him. "Your eagerness pleases me, wife." He pulled Kexen's feet free from his boots and tore off his stockings before tugging the gown completely off. "I only ask for patience while I disrobe to join you."

Kexen leaned back, dressed only in his shift, and watched as his husband stripped off his own clothing with the same speed and economy of motion. Soon, unlike himself, Ben was completely nude. His large cock was standing erect, red and bulging with veins on either side. The sight of it gave him a moment of panic as he remembered the feel of that monstrous thing breaching his hole. He beat down the response, reminding himself that he had Minna's cream to ease the way, even though he dared not suggest they drink her passion-potion, given that they had much of the day still ahead of them.

Something of what he'd felt must have shown on his face because Ben put a reassuring hand on his knee. "Be easy, darling. We are taking matters slowly, remember? I accepted your invitation with only a mild dalliance in mind." He chuckled. "Don't look so disappointed. I promise you'll enjoy it, nevertheless."

Kexen understood that his husband had intended those words to be of comfort, yet they had perversely dashed Kexen's hopes for the afternoon. He hadn't anticipated being so conflicted, and it did nothing to help his marriage to be that way. *I mustn't show mixed feelings about what I want and trust Ben to take care of me.* Resolved, he allowed Ben to tug him onto his feet long enough to pull back the covers and settle them both onto the mattress. As with before, the man wasted no time claiming his mouth and giving free rein to his passion. He pulled Kexen into his arms as they lay facing each other, slipping his knee between Kexen's legs. The man's hard dick brushed against his hip, and Kexen's arousal chafed under the confines of the thin material that lay between them. When he tried to pull the hem up, Ben's hand was suddenly there, doing it for him, bringing it up waist-level to lie on Kexen's hip. Then the man grabbed both their cocks and clasped them together.

The firmness of the grip and the feel of the heat of the man's dick sent Kexen flying before he had time to revel in the pleasure. He bucked and groaned into his husband's hold as warm cum spurted out of both their dicks and splashed against his stomach. Ben held him tightly as they both rode the climax. Kexen squeezed his husband just as firmly, scratching at his back. When the orgasm subsided, all he could do was lie limp against him. Ben rolled onto his back, bringing Kexen with him so that his head rested against Ben's chest. His husband's heart was beating wildly into Kexen's ear and they both continued to pant. Unable to keep his eyes open, his pretext of needing rest was replaced with an actual desire to sleep. He slid under with the sure feeling that his husband was with him and keeping him close and with a half-formed plan to prod his husband to greater passion swirling inside his head.

* * * *

"Lady Tentrees, would you do me the honor of taking a spin with me? I think your husband has had enough skating for today."

Ben's grip on Kexen's hand tightened, although whether it was some kind of warning or due to his continued fear of falling was hard to say. The way Ben leaned against the wooden railing erected around the rink, Kexen was inclined to believe it was the latter. His husband hadn't been kidding when he'd said he had no experience with ice skating. And he had no aptitude for it, that was for sure. As good as Kexen was at the sport, it had proven impossible to teach the man how to skate on his own. It had been enough to merely keep him upright.

Ben was eyeing Prince Rupert with banked annoyance. The queen's preening betrothed was excellent on the ice, and the fact that he'd asked to take Kexen for a spin must be particularly galling for a man as prideful as Ben. Still, he gave the other man a smile and held Kexen's hand aloft. "Please, my dear, take the prince up on his offer. He will provide you with far more fun than I could."

Kexen gave his husband a hard look. If he hadn't known him as well as he did, he would have sworn that he was sincere. At that moment, he appreciated how much a diplomat had to hide his true feelings. "Very well. If you're sure?"

By way of answer, Ben let go of his hand and waved toward the center of the ice. "I would be delighted to see how good you are, darling."

There was nothing to argue against, so Kexen held out his hand to the prince and allowed the man to lead him away. Almost immediately, Rupert had him by the side of his waist, leading him around the rink. The man's movements were graceful, and it was easy for Kexen to sync up with his steps. Their speed increased before Rupert started twirling him as they went. Kexen had never skated in a dress before. He loved the way his skirts billowed out with his movement. He was glad to have chosen his peplum coat instead of the heavier and longer cape. Laughter escaped him before he knew it, but he tempered his joy somewhat when they passed Ben. His poor husband was holding on to the railing with both hands now, trying to look at ease and failing miserably.

"You are a marvelous partner, Lady Tentrees. Let's pick up the pace, shall we?"

"Why not?" Kexen was as much a part of the mission as Ben. If skating with Rupert enhanced their visibility, then it was all to the good. Plus, it was exhilarating fun, and as he whipped around the rink, he felt almost as much joy as he'd experienced in Ben's arms early that afternoon. The day was proving to be glorious, and he felt sure they would succeed at both diplomacy and their marriage.

* * * *

"Your wife is a marvelous skater."

Ben turned his head only so much as was necessary to see the woman speaking to him. He very much feared that any amount of movement was going to land him on his ass. That humiliation was not to be born. He was surprised by who he saw. "Madam Apothecary?" While they had not yet been introduced, he recognized who she was from Kexen's description alone.

The lovely older woman, who was clearly not a native to the Iron Shore as Kexen had remarked, graced him with an endearing smile. "Yes, that is my title. I prefer to be called Minna by my friends, and as Kexen's husband, I count you as one. I hope you will do the same in time."

"Of course, Madam." One foot slipped and it took a moment for him to regain his balance. "Forgive me," he said with a grimace. "I am not a natural on the ice."

The woman chuckled daintily. "I share your affliction. As much as my dear late husband tried to teach me, I find this activity to be highly dangerous to my dignity." She held out her hand. "Come. No one expects you to linger there. Where are your boots?"

The idea of getting the skates off and reclaiming his equilibrium was tempting, but he hated the idea of letting Kexen and Rupert out of his sight. "Thank you, but I prefer to wait for my wife." He slid his gaze to the left as the couple sped past him.

Minna dropped her hand. "I understand. You are protective of your wife, no matter the circumstances, and that it to your credit. Nothing untoward can occur, however, given the setting, and the prince is an affable man...for the most part."

Ben refocused on her. "Should I be concerned by his interest?" His tone came out sharper than he'd intended.

The woman didn't seem to notice—or, at least, didn't take offense. "Not that I'm aware of. He's a terrible flirt, has even tried it on with me, if you can believe such a thing." She shook her head with a grin. "My caution simply stems from the fact that he is a member of the Iron Shore royalty and, as such, can be entirely too intent on his own wants and dismissive of others'. I was very gentle when turning him away, and he tried only the once. And I don't mean to alarm you. Besides, staying in the queen's good graces includes being respectful and somewhat submissive to her betrothed's wishes. There really was no other choice but to allow Kexen to skate with him."

"I am aware." He watched as his wife and Rupert made complicated patterns with their feet as they whirled around the other skaters. They really were remarkably well-suited in this endeavor. And Minna was right. There was no need to worry about something untoward happening in this public setting in particular, especially as the queen was out there as well, changing partners frequently.

"I suppose I should get off, as you suggested, Madam, before I humiliate myself." Tearing his gaze away from his wife, he accepted the apothecary's hand and gladly traded the leg-breaking skates for his sturdy boots.

* * * *

"I'm almost ready."

Ben paced behind his wife's maid as the woman finished up with Kexen's hair. "There is no need to hurry. You're not late. I'm early."

His wife looked at him through the reflection of the vanity mirror. "You didn't need to take the time to wash, that's all. I don't think I've ever spent so much time in the bath. The skating was exhilarating, though." He turned his face this way and that. "And my cheeks are still flushed enough from the cold that I don't need to apply any rouge."

Ben stopped and stared back at him. "You never need face paint, darling. You are beautiful without enhancement."

Kexen rolled his eyes. "Thank you, but you know nothing of how women of this or any other court judge others when it comes to such matters." He reached into his new bowl that now sat on the vanity top and took out a yellow garnet necklace that Ben had given him. It was the perfect complement to the golden-hued gown he wore. Ben started to say as much when a memory clicked inside his head. He went to pick up the bowl. "I know where I've seen this pattern before. I can't believe I didn't recognize it immediately, given how much I scrutinized my first sighting of it." Perhaps he should be worried about his own tiredness and not Kexen's.

Kexen turned his head while Euphemia secured the necklace around his neck. "Where?"

"The queen showed me the original throne room of her dynasty. Its age pre-dates much of the history we have about the Iron Shore." He held up the bowl. "This pattern was carved on the arms and back of the chair."

Kexen turned to him fully. "Was it made out of the same wood?"

Ben shook his head as his mind worked to make sense of it all. "No. Age had darkened the color, but it was still recognizable as the same type as you see in the very panels of this room. It's the design that tells a story."

"I'm sorry, Ben, but I'm being a bit dense about all this. I don't understand the point you are making."

That statement caught his attention. Putting the bowl down, he peered into Kexen's eyes. "Your mind is as sharp as anyone on the king's council. It is I who am slow to understand the significance of this, given what I already know."

"Which is…?"

Ben paced away, his mind whirling with the new facts. "You've seen how much Magnus favors the Iron Shore people?"

Kexen stood as well. "Yes. He looks as much like a relative of the queen as Rupert does."

"Exactly, which confirms that the rumors of Far Isle being populated long ago by Iron Shore people are correct. The issue now is whether there was a migration or colonization."

"I don't think I know the distinction."

"If those ancient Iron Shore people settled in a place that was devoid of people, then they would have established a new homeland for their kind. If they found other people there and took over the place, that would make them conquerors."

Kexen threw up his hands. "I'm still lost. I can see how Magnus' claim of common ancestry might give him an advantage with the trade agreement, but what does the rest of it have to do with the present?"

Ben stopped and stared at the floor. "Likely nothing. I just find it interesting that a pattern that appears to reflect royalty here found its way to Far Isle. And also, it's curious that a people originating from the Iron Shore would have formed a constitutional monarchy when an absolute one is still observed in their country of origin."

Kexen tapped his slipper-covered toe. "I don't know what that means, either."

"It means that while they have a hereditary monarch, they also have codified law that cannot be changed by the will of any particular one. The people choose a governing council that *can* change the law if the people will it so but serve mostly to ensure that the monarch obeys them."

"What an odd system. And to whom does the military answer?"

"Ultimately, the people, through the control of the council."

Kexen raised his eyebrows. "That is surprising. It's a wonder such a system of governing gained traction and remains."

Ben grimaced. "That is the prevailing reaction, my darling, from diplomats of my acquaintance. It is an interesting puzzle. I wonder if people native to that area instilled the idea into the relocated Iron Shore travelers."

"Your pardon, my lord," Euphemia interjected. "If it's of any help to you, I can relay that Envoy Magnus' entourage looks nothing like him. They are darker in all aspects. I've never seen the like before, yet it's clear to me that the Iron Shore people are used to seeing them through trade."

Baldrick entered the room and the conversation. "My sister is right, my lord."

"Indeed?" Ben found the information fascinating and mentally kicked himself for not looking into the people surrounding Magnus. "That may mean that Magnus is descended from Iron Shore colonists that at some point ended up being integrated into the local population and their customs."

"That's not my understanding of how conquering works," Kexen observed.

"Nor mine."

Kexen came over and rested his fingers on Ben's arm. "Who benefits from this information?"

Ben took Kexen's hand and wrapped his arm around his own. "I honestly have no idea. I may be simply performing mental masturbation." When his wife raised his eyebrows, he explained. "It's an expression we diplomats use." He pressed a kiss against Kexen's brow. "It's a beautiful bowl, regardless. Let's go to dinner."

With that, he escorted his wife out of their suite, his thoughts already focused on the evening. Still, in the back of his mind, he couldn't help feeling there was something he was missing.

Chapter Eight

Ben wasn't certain he would survive an entire winter in Amira's palace if the young woman kept up this level of excess. The abundance of food, drink and merriment surely could not be sustained much longer without the denizens of the palace falling into a stupor. He got the impression that the queen was making up for a dreary court under her father's rule. She seemed intent on cramming in a lifetime of excitement into one season. On the other hand, if the point of the evenings' revelry was to weed out the weak, it was diabolical — and a game he was prepared to win. Unlike Magnus, he'd taken to eating and drinking in moderation without calling attention to it. Kexen's recent illness was still a handy excuse to retire early, but that was going to end soon. His wife was demonstrating that he was robust after only a few days of proper eating and rest. Everyone was remarking on it, and the fact that he cut such an alluring figure among the court was, on balance, a great benefit. The next day's planned activity was possibly going to add to that vision. He looked forward to having a good night's sleep. It might be the last time they'd be able to rest for such a long stretch.

He headed into the bedroom. "Kexen, do you hunt?" Because he was already undoing his robe's sash, Ben didn't see his wife until he was halfway to the bed. When he looked up, the spit in his mouth dried and he dropped his hands. "What in the...? My darling, you'll catch a cold dressed thusly." It was a ridiculous thing to say but nothing else intelligible formed in his brain. It had turned to mush at the sight of his wife lounging in the bed, wearing the same sheer nightgown he'd worn on their wedding night. It continued to allow tantalizing glimpses of the silky, pale flesh beneath. Ben's dick, naturally, came into its own, hardening in an instant.

Kexen gave him a heated look while raising one knee. "I'm not worried about that. Your body will keep me warm."

Ben forced his feet to move forward. "I will be honored to aid you in any way you need, but I fear that I am too overcome with the enticement you provide for me to be content with serving as a warming pan."

Kexen smiled coquettishly. "That is my intent—to lure you into marital passion." He sat up. "I know you said you want to take matters slowly, but I don't think I can wait. I want you to claim me completely tonight, Ben."

There was no denying that he wanted that as well. Still, the events of their wedding night loomed large in his mind. He didn't want to make any more mistakes with his bride. The original plan of getting to know each other better, exploring each other's bodies in a measured way, remained safer and more sensible. "I will not risk hurting you again." He kept his voice gentle and sat on the edge of the mattress.

"I'm not afraid of that." Kexen picked up two small glasses of wine from the table next to the bed. He held one out. "This is doctored with Minna's potion. She promises that it will enhance our arousal while relaxing us at the same time. Her ointment will do the rest better than any oil. Will you try them both with me?"

Ben took the proffered glass and first peered into it, then sniffed its contents. There was nothing to detect other than a fairly robust red. "I'm sure Madam Apothecary knows her craft well and has only the best of intentions. However..." He didn't get a chance to finish his thought. His words were cut short by his bride downing the glass in one shot. Ben winced. "Darling, I'm not sure that was the most sensible thing to do."

Kexen merely melted back on a mound of pillows and smiled. "I'm not concerned. You're here to take care of me if I lose control, and if you don't want to drink it, that's fine. I have no doubt that you need no enhancement. In fact, I can see that you don't." Kexen's gaze homed in on Ben's lap.

He didn't need to look as well to know his cock was tenting his small clothes. Putting his glass on the table, he replied, "True enough. A gorgeous young man in my bed is sufficiently stimulating. And why would I risk making my mind fuzzy when I need to treat you with care?"

"I trust you, Ben. And as you can see, I am also eager for you to have me, even without the potion's effect." The sheer material was draped over the boy's erection and although he said it didn't come from what he'd drunk, there was already a sheen to his eyes and his pupils were blown wider than anything Ben had ever seen. If nothing else, his wife wasn't going to be plagued by tension.

He ran his hand up Kexen's leg, gathering the hem of the gown in his fingers as he did so. "I don't intend to rush, darling. It's not only for your sake, either. You won't deny me the pleasure of feasting on your whole body, will you?"

"Oh, Ben." Kexen sighed and went limp, exposing himself and giving Ben complete access.

He wasted no time, using his tongue to trace the path his fingers had made, first on one leg, then the other. There was a sweet taste to the skin, a lotion no doubt applied after his nighttime bath. That simple ministration caused his wife to quiver, making Ben bolder. He began to lap at Kexen's balls while reaching up with his hands to tweak the boy's nipples. His wife's comparatively small stature served Ben well in this endeavor. It took nothing for him to attack various parts of his body simultaneously. He pulled staccato huffs from Kexen by lavishing attention with his tongue on the area surrounding his cock.

With each new touch, Kexen's quivering increased until Ben had to use his larger body to keep his bride in place. His breathing became more labored, panting now as if he'd run full speed. He clenched the sheet beneath him with his fingers and rocked his head back and forth. Ben palmed the shaft that throbbed near his cheek, caressing it with a light touch before gripping it tightly at the base. It wouldn't do for his wife to come too soon. He wanted to time it so that Kexen was riding an orgasm when he was finally breached again by Ben's cock. It was the best way to ensure that only pleasure would be had, not pain.

Kexen moaned and cursed in equal measure, urging Ben to get on with it. Ben let go of the dick long enough to strip his bride of the nightgown and used it as an opportunity to mute his wife with a long, slow kiss. He was careful to hold himself off him, however. Any touch could send him — both of them — over the edge. Kexen tried to nip his tongue while straining upward to reconnect them, earning himself a chuckle. Ben liked the boldness of his wife but was determined to keep command of the situation. He pulled away from those teeth and pressed Kexen onto his back before kissing and sucking down the boy's chest. Clasping his cock once more, he alternated between stroking and choking to keep Kexen on edge. When he reached the abdomen, he lapped the cockhead before taking the shaft into his mouth as much as his fist would allow. For a short while, he stimulated his wife's arousal without letting him come. When Kexen's cries turned into frustration, Ben decided it was time to claim his bride as he should have done that first night.

He pressed against the backs of Kexen's legs, bending his torso and exposing his hole. Using saliva, Ben tested the resistance of the puckered ring. It was a relief to find it already somewhat pliable, the effect of the potion, no doubt. But it wouldn't be sufficient to ease the way for his cock. He remembered Kexen had spoken of a cream, and there on the table sat a squat ceramic pot. Ben used his own thighs to keep Kexen in place while reaching for it, then tested the concoction between his thumb and forefinger. It held a faintly sweet smell and was far thicker than any oil he might have used. Although he was confident the apothecary held no bad intent, he still wasn't willing to simply slather his wife with the unknown substance. Instead, he tried it on himself, coating his cock with a thin layer. At first, it felt like nothing, then the heat came and a tingling feeling. It wasn't unpleasant, quite the contrary. He could see how it would elevate the sexual experience.

"Ben, please." There was a begging tone to Kexen's voice.

"Apologies, darling. I was just testing out Madam Apothecary's cream. I am sure you will enjoy it."

With that, Ben wasted no time in dipping two fingers into the pot this time and slathering it around Kexen's ever-more-pliant hole. He tested the welcome his dick might receive by slowly inserting first one finger, then another. Kexen's tight heat sucked them in easily. His hole clenched around them as Ben gently fucked the channel to open it, and when he turned and crooked the tips to rub against the boy's prostate, Kexen nearly levitated off the mattress. There was more begging and writhing under this touch, so much so that Ben realized he couldn't wait much longer. Still, he had to be sure that his wife was ready for him, so he worked the channel of his ass some more, adding in a third finger to stretch it. When he felt little resistance, he pulled them out and positioned himself between his bride's legs. He held his cock against the hole and slowly pushed himself in.

It was nothing like the first time. The memory of that was fleeting and overwhelmed with the pleasure of being mounted by his husband. The potion had made him relaxed and almost giddy. The cream had loosened him, even as its tingling heat sent his arousal to greater heights. The slight burn of being stretched wide surprisingly added to his enjoyment. When Ben bottomed out and went still, Kexen almost yelled with frustration. He wanted to be fucked — hard and fast — and used every bit of his voice and body to urge his husband to give him what he craved. Attentive as Ben was, he didn't require much prodding. Bracing himself on his elbows, he loomed over Kexen and began to thrust.

Kexen closed his eyes and groaned from the force of it. He had to clench the sheet beneath him as he bounced from the assault. Instinctively he wrapped his legs around his husband's waist to both anchor himself and to pull Ben closer to him. The man's warm breath fanned his face, proof of how much effect he was having on him, too. Neither of them was going to last long at the pace Ben had set. And when Ben reached between their sweating bodies and merely touched Kexen's dick again, he came with a force that made him scream. His suddenly weak legs fell open and it felt as if his body tried to float off the bed, held in place only by the connection of Ben's cock inside him and the larger body covering his. A flood of warmth and a masculine cry of completion had Kexen coming again. His world spun and he must have passed out, because the next thing he knew Ben was kneeling next to him, stroking his cheek.

"Darling, are you still with me? Open your eyes more, please. Let me see that you're all right."

Kexen gave his husband a lazy grin. "I feel as if I died and have been reborn."

Ben frowned. "No more of that potion for you. Here… Have some water." He lifted Kexen's head and held a glass to his lips. "This should help."

It was deliciously cool, and his mouth was dry and his tongue thick. He drank the whole of it before lying back onto the pillows. That was when he realized he was under the covers. "How long was I out?"

Ben slid off the bed, magnificently nude, his cock swinging between his legs, not quite soft again. "Long enough that I considered calling for Madam Apothecary." He dimmed the lamps and returned. "As I said, no more potion. I can arouse you without it," he added before sliding into bed and gathering Kexen close.

The skin-to-skin contact was delicious. Kexen wiggled as close to his husband as he could and lay his head on his chest. "I have no doubt. The cream was excellent help, though, don't you think?"

"Agreed. It's far more effective that mere oil." Ben paused and tightened his hold. "Are you all right?"

"Wonderful," Kexen assured him on a sigh. "There is a sweet ache where your cock invaded, no pain and only a promise of more pleasure to come."

Ben kissed the top of his head. "I am gratified to hear that. This is what it should have been like from the beginning."

"Hush." Kexen hugged him with one arm. "No more about that. It is done and over. This is the memory to replace it."

"You are a very understanding wife."

"I like to think so." Kexen added a smile to his words. There were others caught in his throat, ones that had come to him unbidden and unexpectedly. *I'm falling in love with him.* It seemed obvious and silly at the same time. He dared not speak of it out loud, certainly. Perhaps this kind of intense emotion came to one simply through the physical act of sex. He needed to sit with it for a while and decide whether what he felt for his husband was real or not.

Ben kissed him on the top of his head once more. "It is late. We need to go to sleep if we are going to have the energy for the hunt."

"Mm-m." Kexen's eyes flew open. "Wait! What?"

Ben's chest rose and fell quickly. "Damnation, I never got the chance to tell you. I was *distracted*. In any event, the queen has called for a hunt tomorrow first thing in the morning. We'll eat a full breakfast in the field. You'd think given her father's accident she'd be off hunting—but apparently not. We'll be seeking mountain elk, very docile creatures and easily shot once they are located. I suppose it makes for mostly a jaunty ride through the woods. You do hunt, do you not?"

Kexen wrinkled his nose. "I don't like killing things, but yes, I know how to hunt. Almost all Outer Vale people do. I mostly enjoy it for as you say, the fun of the ride. I like to gallop through the trees and take jumps over hedges and streams. I simply won't take a bow with me. And I commissioned an adorable green riding habit with black velvet piping and fur trim for my trousseau. I'm happy to have an opportunity to show it off."

Ben chuckled. "I'm glad you have a reason to look forward to it. It won't take more than half the day, and I imagine it will be quite tame." He yawned loudly. "Now, close your eyes, darling, and if you are very good and get your rest, maybe I'll have time to fuck you again in the morning."

Kexen groaned and smacked his husband's abdomen. "You beast! How am I to sleep now?" His cock was already stirring once more.

Ben patted his ass. "Try, darling, try." There was another loud yawn and Ben went silent.

Kexen snuggled against him and let the remnants of the potion make him float away.

* * * *

Kexen refused the groom's offer to help him mount his horse. Even with an apron skirt covering his breaches, he was still capable of hoisting himself onto the saddle. His riding skills were among those he prided the most, and he looked forward to showing them off to both Ben and Amira's court. As he settled his ass, he could feel the lasting effect of Ben's early morning fuck. Unlike after their wedding night, this lingering ache gave him satisfaction, not pain. He had shared that most precious part of himself with his husband in glorious pleasure and couldn't wait to do so again. He was glad he'd safeguarded this one physical act to share with a man he prized above all others. It was no wonder that his affection for Ben had morphed into love. Or at least, that is how he interpreted the way his heart stuttered and his stomach flip-flopped from the sight of the man. That was especially so with the backdrop of the early morning light glistening off the snow-covered ground as Ben approached him, decked out all in black. The man cut quite a figure on horseback.

Kexen smiled in welcome, even as he responded to his mount's efforts at testing his control. The Iron Shore people chose the horses they bought well. They were broad, sturdy beasts with long hair hanging from their fetlocks. They seemed well-suited for the cold and treacherous ground. And like all their kind, they would try to get away with whatever their rider permitted. With well-practiced movements, Kexen let his know that he was the one in command. The horse tossed its head and snorted before settling down. "It's a beautiful day for a hunt."

Ben nodded. "It is, but I must say I'm glad we partook of toast and tea before leaving our suite. I don't want you to become too chilled or hungry from riding in this cold."

Kexen waved his hand from his fur headband down to his thick boots. "I'm fine. You worry too much, husband."

Ben's expression turned serious. "That is not possible where you're concerned. I can see, however, you have control over your mount. That's one less thing I will fuss about. I'll stay behind you just in case you need help, though."

Kexen eyed the crossbow slung over the man's shoulders. "Really, Ben, how do you expect to hunt if you do? And it's not necessary for you to watch over me. I can sit a horse as well as anyone here, and I met Minna as she was mounting up. She says she enjoys the exercise and is on hand in case anyone gets hurt."

"I trust Madam Apothecary can tend to injuries, but my duty is to make sure you don't require her services. Besides, I don't care if I get off a shot."

"Truly, Tentrees?" Magnus had come up behind Ben without Kexen noticing. "What is the point of hunting if not to seek bringing down the most prized prey? I, for one, intend to ride as close to the queen as possible."

Ben turned to look at the Far Isle envoy. "I wish you good luck, then. I'm sure the queen will be delighted if you upstage her in a kill." Kexen winced inwardly at the barb, although he couldn't fault his husband for it. Diplomacy was a type of war, and Magnus had started the veiled confrontation.

A look of anger slid past Magnus' face before he regained his pleasant demeanor. "What I do is for her glory, not mine. I'll dedicate my kill to her, and she is a woman who appreciates manly efforts. I'm sure she sees your solicitousness of your wife equally as impressive." The man's tone implied otherwise.

"I would assume so," Ben replied coolly. "Taking care of one's family is an important mark of a man's character. I expect you've left your own wife in good hands back home."

"I have no wife." Magnus' tone was dismissive.

"I'm sorry to hear that. Having the comfort of Lady Tentrees by my side is a great source of joy." He turned his head to wink at Kexen out of Magnus' sight. There was an undercurrent to Ben going down this domestic track. He was needling the Far Isle envoy but also extracting information from the man effortlessly.

For what purpose, Kexen wasn't sure, but he knew to go along with it. "I likewise value my husband's protection and company."

Magnus stared down his nose at him. "Really, Lady Tentrees? I was under the impression that Prince Rupert shared more of your interests than your husband." With that smart remark, the man whirled his horse around and cantered closer to the queen and her entourage. He blended seamlessly with the Iron Shore people.

"Well," Kexen exclaimed in a soft voice, "it didn't take long for his true colors to show. What were you fishing for with him, anyway?"

Ben rubbed a gloved finger over his chin before answering. "I have a theory about what his plan here might be, and learning that he is unencumbered by a wife feeds into it — too well, as it happens."

Before Kexen could ask a follow-up question, the Master of the Hounds sounded his horn. The dozen large, shaggy dogs milling about started barking and took off in a pack into the woods. The humans followed suit, with the queen riding behind the Master of the Hounds and everyone else ranging out after her. Kexen started toward the back but soon overtook many of the hunters simply by his riding skill alone. It was exhilarating to canter into the tree line, dodging obstacles while following the baying hounds as they tracked the scent of their prey. He pushed his mount as fast as it could go once he got a sense of its sure-footedness.

They flew easily over the first stream they came to. Kexen laughed with abandon, the most carefree he'd felt since his journey had begun. When they entered a clear area, he could see Ben out of the corner of his eye, keeping pace with him. He couldn't help urging his mount to greater speed, simply to force Ben to keep up with him. If they'd been alone, he could have anticipated what delightful price he might pay for being caught. As it was, he could only imagine it happening, and that was fun enough. Only a short while ago, he'd feared he might never find the physical side of marriage enjoyable. A weight had lifted from him now that he knew he would.

As they approached the higher elevation of the forest, the Master of the Hounds blew his horn again to signal that their quarry had been spotted. Hunters were spread out over a significant distance. Kexen could only see flashes of them as they passed by among the trees. Everyone was intent on getting ahead for a chance to shoot. There was another blow, then intense braying by the hounds. Over the crackling of hoofs on the forest floor, he could hear the thwacks of bolts being loosened and hitting targets. Then there was a high-pitched scream—not a human one, nor did it come from one of the poor, dumb beasts that they hunted. It had been a horse that had made the terrible sound. He knew it for what it was instantly and from where it came. Pulling tight on the reins, Kexen whirled his mount around.

"Ben!" Kexen watched in horror as his husband's horse dropped to its side, an arrow sticking from its throat, blood spurting and the poor thing wailing its death cries. It was horrible in and of itself, but the worst was that Ben was leaping off the saddle to keep from being crushed. His head hit a nearby tree with a sickening thud.

Kexen didn't waste his breath calling his husband's name again. Instead, he screamed for Minna as he dismounted and rushed to Ben's side. He fell to his knees and touched Ben's cheek. "My love, are you hurt?"

Ben's eyes were closed, and he gave no answer. He was breathing, however, so surely that was a good sign, and there didn't appear to be any blood under his head. Hunters started to gather around them. Kexen paid them no mind other than to call for Minna again. The woman appeared finally and knelt beside him.

"Have you tried to move him?"

"No."

"Good. We don't know if there is an injury to his neck that will be made worse by doing so without first stabilizing his torso."

"He hit his head against the tree." The memory of the sound roiled Kexen's stomach. He put a hand to it and forced himself to ignore the feeling. Throwing up wasn't going to help Ben.

Minna touched the area around it. "There isn't any noticeable blood." She then began to gently feel Ben's body from head to toe, looking for injuries, no doubt.

Kexen watched her anxiously until he heard a low moan. "Ben?" His husband's eyes fluttered open. "Minna, he's coming to."

The woman peered into Ben's face. "Where are you hurt, Lord Tentrees?"

Ben winced and lifted his hand briefly before letting it flop down again. Kexen wrapped his fingers around it and was buoyed by Ben clasping them in turn. "My head is pounding, but otherwise I think my wounds are mostly to my dignity." He grimaced. "The horse?"

"It's dead," Kexen replied. "It was shot through the neck with a bolt."

"I remember it stumbling and starting to fall. I couldn't quite tell why. How in the gods' names did it happen? We're too far from the head of the hunt."

"That's a very good question." Furious now that his worst fears had been allayed, Kexen whipped his head around to stare at the hunters who had gathered. Far in the back was the queen, Master Prime Minister, Prince Rupert and Magnus. They had been well ahead of them, so couldn't have done it. The others, though... "Who is responsible for this?" Kexen let his rage show through his face.

No one stepped forward to confess. Of course, they didn't. Kexen was on the verge of shouting the question out again...this time with more *feeling*, when Minna's touch to his arm to stop him.

"You will learn nothing here and now," she said in a low voice. "We should concentrate on getting your husband into bed so that I can exam him more thoroughly. I need a chaise!" she called out.

"No." This from Ben. "I don't need carrying." To prove his point, he slowly sat up. "I need a fresh mount, that is all."

Kexen wanted to argue with the stubborn man. There was no telling what injury he might be suffering without knowing it. But he understood that Amira's court was watching — some with pity, others with glee over the drama. Magnus surely was hoping Ben would look weak over this. For the sake of the mission and Ben's pride, Kexen decided to help his husband achieve what he wanted. There would be plenty of time later to berate him over it.

Putting his arms around Ben's chest, he said, "Let me help you. You can ride with me back to the palace."

"Thank you, darling." More quietly, he added, "You are a treasure."

Kexen tucked the compliment aside to enjoy later. It was a struggle, but with Minna's help, Ben managed to stand. Kexen kept hold of him as they approached Kexen's mount, which one of the groomers on the hunt had wisely held the reins to. Then there was the even more difficult challenge of helping Ben into the saddle. Once he was steady, Kexen got on behind him and took the reins. Ben was already holding them to demonstrate to one and all that he was in control. Kexen knew better. The man needed help and it was up to Kexen to give it as surreptitiously as possible. It was awkward to sit in this order, given how broad Ben was compared to Kexen's arms. But the optics of a man like Ben riding pillion was something to be avoided, as well. Besides, Kexen had no doubt he could get them safely back to the palace, even leading from behind. With his head held high and his gaze as confident as he could make it, he started the long, slow journey back.

Chapter Nine

"I wish to repeat my objection to this," Ben said.

Kexen finished checking himself out in the mirror before responding. He'd purposely chosen a virginal light blue gown with three-quarter sleeves that had long lace cuffs, a high ruff collar and lots of flounces. Mistress Camilla had insisted on Kexen having at least one dress that was as girlish as possible. This evening seemed like the perfect occasion to make use of it.

He turned to Ben, who lay on top of the bed with a scowl on his face. "It is duly noted, as it has been each of the million times you've made it."

"You exaggerate, wife."

"And you call me 'wife' any time you're annoyed or being stern. You should know I'm not intimidated by it." Kexen approached the bed to study what he considered a too-pale face. "You heard what Minna said about head injuries being tricky. Spending the evening in bed instead of making merry with the queen is a sensible precaution. The mission will not benefit from your becoming incapacitated because you did too much too soon after the fall." He didn't add that he was not yet free of the fear that Ben would die from the accident. *If it was an accident.*

"I accept Madam Apothecary's advice and will stay in this bed like the invalid that I am *not.* However, I still dislike the idea of your going to supper without me. There is no need."

Kexen rolled his eyes. "Are you sure you're all right, because you seem to keep forgetting that we've had this conversation before. We can't afford to give Magnus even one evening alone with the queen and her court at this point. It's bad enough that he felled the biggest buck during the hunt and, if servants' gossip is to be believed, presented the carcass to the queen with much charming fanfare. We don't need to give him an opportunity to whisper in her ear about us.

"Hopefully my presence will do more to demonstrate the hardiness and seriousness of Moorcondia than any honeyed words ever will. I'm not afraid, Ben, and this is why you married me, after all. I know how to navigate the social politics of a court."

Ben's expression eased a bit and a look entered his eyes. "That's not the only reason why I married you." He patted the mattress beside him. "Come here to me, and I will explain better."

"Gods!" With a shake of his head, Kexen headed for the doorway to the sitting room. Baldrick stood like a sentinel there, silently listening. "Take good care of your master and make sure he stays in bed. Sit on him, if you have to," he added before blowing a kiss to his husband.

He ignored Ben's continued entreaties and sailed out of their suite. Once in the hallway, he took a few deep breaths to calm his nerves before heading into what he considered unfriendly terrain. *You can do this. You are Kexen of the Outer Vale and Lady Tentrees. There is nothing you can't handle.* With that inner bolster of encouragement, he went to supper trying to hide the feeling that he was heading to his doom.

* * * *

"What a shame your husband has to miss such a festive evening."

Kexen smiled at Prince Rupert as the man led him around the outer edge of the ballroom in a slow waltz. "It is, but there's always another party tomorrow, is there not? And really, I'm just relieved that his accident wasn't more serious."

The prince held his waist more tightly as the tempo of the music picked up. "Yes, terrible. Nothing like that has ever happened before on a hunt."

"It's too bad that whoever made the mistake hasn't come forward to confess. My husband would forgive them, naturally." He tried to put some distance between their bodies. His heart had sunk when the prince had asked for such an intimate dance. Kexen had done a good job of fending off other men and sticking to the more boisterous reels. But one didn't refuse royalty when they insisted, so here he was as the evening was winding down, in Rupert's exuberant embrace.

"I'm sure the Master of the Hounds will determine what happened. It's nothing you need to worry about." He leaned in close to Kexen's face. "It would be a pity for your beauty to be marred by frown lines."

Kexen leaned back, which was when he realized that they were not only on the fringe of the dance floor but actually on a balcony. The cool air on the back of his neck was welcome—the seclusion, not so much. No stranger to leading in a partner's dance, he tried to move them in the opposite direction. Rupert's strength was unassailable, however, and determination showed through his eyes. It took only a few steps for them to be past the ballroom entrance and into the one for the hallway that servants used to ferry food. It was late and the tables were cleared, so there was no one about, not even guards, given that no one of importance was expected to be there.

Kexen planted his feet. "We seem to be in the wrong place, Your Highness."

Rupert's answering smile was alarming. "On the contrary, Lady Tentrees, we are exactly where we both want to be…away from prying eyes." He used his arms to tug Kexen closer.

Kexen dropped all pretense of civility and sliding his arms between their bodies, pushed hard against the man's chest. "Your Highness, you are mistaken in my interest. I am married, and you are betrothed—to your *queen*."

Rupert was too heavy to force back. He leered down at him. "She holds no appeal for me and likes to bed other men, anyway. I'm sure she'll be lying under Magnus shortly, as she's already done. Your husband's prudish faithfulness to you is not helping the Moorcondian cause. He should focus on getting under the queen's skirts if he wants that treaty, and you, my dear, should do the same with me." He backed Kexen up until he was against a wall.

"What? Try to get under *your* skirts?"

Rupert chuckled. "Such a clever tongue. I like that. And your female mode of dress is surprisingly fetching. Let's see what treasures you're hiding." He slid his hands along Kexen's hip and began to bunch up the material of his gown. "So many layers. You wear your gown like armor. I like the challenge of working to find what I want." That was all he said before slamming his mouth onto Kexen's and, at the same time, squeezing one of his pecs.

The time for diplomacy was clearly at an end. Kexen allowed only a moment of regret for the damage he might do to the mission — before he drove his knee into Rupert's balls. The man jerked back with wide eyes before bending in pain, his mouth open in a silent scream. Smart man, he no more wanted to call attention to them than Kexen did. And while Rupert was in such a vulnerable position, Kexen punched him in the face to be sure to keep him incapacitated. The prince lay writhing on the ground in the semi-darkness. None of the other members of court who remained at the party had come nearby on the balcony. That could change quickly. It might be that this was a favorite place for a tryst. Kexen needed to leave immediately.

Wiping his mouth of the man's saliva, Kexen leaned over him, careful to stay out of reach: "I trust you'll stay quiet about all this. I will. This treaty is more important to both of our countries than your dick or my honor."

Kexen didn't get an answer and didn't expect one. He raced away from Rupert until he entered the main hallway where guards were stationed and slowed down. He passed the men with slow, serene steps, using the time to get himself under control. As much as Rupert's actions bothered him, it was important not to give away anything to Ben. He'd meant what he'd said about the treaty. The whole ugly affair would be his and the prince's secret. Maybe when he and Ben were old and gray, he'd tell his husband what had happened — but not now.

The suite was quiet when he opened the door, leading him to hope that Ben was asleep. But he wasn't. Instead Kexen found him lying on top of the bed covers and propped against pillows. He was much as Kexen had left him, except now he had a book in his hand. Plus, Baldrick and Euphemia were gone, which suited him fine. He wasn't up to keeping a serene pretense for a lot of people. Ben would be hard enough.

Ben looked up at him the moment Kexen entered the room. "I'm glad to see you back this early."

Kexen put his hands behind his back to keep from fidgeting. His nerves were not as steady as he'd thought. "Is it? Early, I mean?" He looked around. "Where's my maid? I want to get out of this sweltering dress." He meant it as a diversion to give himself more of a chance to calm down.

"I dismissed the servants for the night. Their hovering was driving me mad. I can help you. I'm not an invalid, and my headache is actually gone."

Kexen walked closer to the bed. "That's Minna's medicine at work."

"I suppose so…" Ben frowned, then sat bolt upright. "What happened to your bodice?"

"What do you mean?" Kexen looked down at his own chest and saw that a piece of the fabric had been ripped away from his collar. Gods, he hadn't noticed. It must have happened when Rupert had first crumpled. "Oh, it's nothing." He pressed his hand against the damage. "I must have snagged it on something."

Ben was off the bed like a shot. "Don't lie to me!" He studied Kexen's face with an intensity that scared him. Ben's gaze lingered on Kexen's lips and, like with the dress, he hadn't considered what evidence might be on display from Rupert's brutal kiss.

Kexen took a step back. "I need a bath. I'm fine. Nothing happened. Please, go back to bed."

Ben was not to be dissuaded, however. "Who did it?" When Kexen shook his head, Ben asked again, louder now and furiously, "Who?"

Concerned that his husband suspected him of infidelity, Kexen couldn't help but go on the defensive. "I invited no attention."

Ben made a visible effort to calm down. "I have no doubt of that. My anger is not directed at you, and I'm sorry if I made you worry otherwise."

"You didn't. Not really. I simply don't want to discuss this right now." *Not ever.* "I'm tired and want to bathe and go to sleep. I'm not hurt, Ben."

"I'm glad to know that. I would never want you to be, and now I know that I don't have to kill anyone, merely beat the shit out of them." The calm way he said the words was more alarming than anything.

Kexen grabbed Ben by the arms. "Please, let's just go to bed."

Ben smiled and, using the edge of his forefinger, raised Kexen's chin to deliver a sweet kiss. "A. Name. You will obey me in this, Kexen," he added sternly.

Kexen feared he might cry for a moment before he sniffed back that useless reaction. It was obvious that his husband was not going to let this go. With trepidation, he submitted. "Rupert."

Ben took a deep breath and squared his shoulders. "I see. Where did this happen?"

"At the end of the service corridor that runs along the ballroom and opens onto the balcony." Kexen licked his lips. "No one saw and I...I kneed him in the balls."

Ben smiled grimly. "Did you now? Very resourceful of you, darling."

"And I punched him so he might still be lying on the floor in agony. Isn't that enough?"

"Not in the least. Go to bed, darling. I'll be back as soon as circumstances allow." So saying, the man calmly pulled on half boots but didn't otherwise change out of the casual shirt and trousers he'd been wearing since returning from the hunt. With his hair down, he looked positively wild.

And yet, Kexen had to try to stop his husband from doing something as foolish as fighting with the queen's betrothed. "Ben, don't do this—or at least wait until morning when you've had a chance to cool down." He chased Ben into the sitting room. "Please, think of the mission."

At the outer door, Ben turned to look at him. "The mission be damned. Stay here," he added before striding out.

Kexen stood staring, trying to quell his mounting panic. "*Fuck that.*" Then he chased after his husband.

Ben was not known for being hotheaded. Quite the contrary. He prided himself on being measured in his approaches and reactions to all manner of situations. And still he wanted to slam Rupert's head into the nearest wall once he got his hands on the man. Something inside him had snapped when he'd seen not the ripped bodice but Kexen's lips. Fabric could be torn for all kinds of reasons, but swollen lips and smeared paint told only one tale. That transgression against his wife would not stand. It didn't matter that the boy was capable of taking care of himself. Ben wasn't surprised at how Kexen had stopped the assault, yet it could have gone the other way just as easily. Rupert was taller and stronger than Kexen. If Kexen had been a bit slower or Rupert more alert...well, it didn't bear thinking about. Kexen was safe. Now it was down to Ben to make sure that Rupert understood his grave mistake and that he would get no other chances to repeat it.

He passed a few denizens of the palace as they made their way to their suites or card rooms. Given his dishevelment, their glances at him were not a surprise. He paid them no mind, his focus on his destination. Part of him hoped Rupert would have slunk off to his bed. Taking the man to task in the strongest possible way was not, as Kexen had pointed out, going to aid the success of the mission. The stronger part of Ben, however — the one in which he held his feelings as a husband — was eager for the confrontation now. He wanted to return to his marital bed, take his wife in his arms and assure him that there was nothing to fear. His steps faltered a moment as he pictured Kexen and allowed the depth of his feeling for the boy to well up. He cared for him more strongly than he'd expected. *I love him?* Yes, very possibly and he'd explore that later, once he'd reduced Rupert to a quivering mess.

The service corridor was quiet and darkened the farther into it he went. In the dimness, he spied a figure on the floor and knew a moment's satisfaction that Kexen had indeed laid Rupert low. But that feeling morphed into alarm when he got close enough to see that Rupert wasn't merely stunned. He was dead. A black pool spread from his crumpled body and a blade stuck in his chest gleamed from the moonlight streaming in from the open balcony doors. He was careful to not touch anything, even as he tried to confirm that the man really had been stabbed. Then there was a crash and a scream.

Ben whipped his head in the direction behind him and saw that a serving girl had come from one of the side doors to the ballroom. She'd dropped her tray and was now raising the roof with her caterwauling. And, of course, everyone within hearing distance came running to the scene. On one side were soldiers with their swords in hand. On the other, streaming from the balcony, were those members of the court who had lingered in the ballroom. Everyone skidded to a halt, their eyes on him. Ben held up his hands to show that he held no weapon and was no threat to anyone there.

"I found him like this."

Master Prime Minister pushed through the crowd to kneel beside Rupert's body, unheeding of the blood there. The man looked up at Ben. "This is a Moorcondian blade. I recognize the markings on the hilt."

Is it? Ben looked closer at it. Someone had thought to turn up the lamps on the walls so he could see clearly from where he stood. Of course, it was. He'd been set up very neatly, although how someone had gotten Rupert to play along was hard to imagine. Rupert had been an idiot, so naturally he'd probably been easy to fool. Then again, he might have simply given others an opening to put a plan in action that had been waiting for the right time. Either way, Ben was in trouble. That was doubly apparent when the queen also pushed her way to her betrothed, and with a wail, threw herself onto his body. Magnus stood behind her, staring at Ben with a smile on his face.

"Let me through."

Ben's heart sank as Kexen threaded past the soldiers to stand at Ben's side. "I did not leave him in this condition," he whispered.

"I know." To the larger audience, Ben reiterated, "Prince Rupert was already slain when I came upon him."

Master Prime Minister rose to his feet. "Why would you or Prince Rupert come here? Did you lure him?" His gaze switched to Kexen. "Or did someone else?"

Ben's blood turned to ice. He needed the focus to stay on him. "I admit I was seeking the prince and thought he might be here because this is where he attacked my wife." Naturally, the answer also bolstered the suspicion that he'd killed the man. There was no hope for it, because lies would always catch you up.

"That is why you killed him," Master Prime Minister pronounced with obvious glee.

"I did not!"

"A Moorcondian blade did the deed."

"That's as may be, but it's not *my* knife...or Lady Tentrees'," he added. "Not that my wife is in the habit of carrying arms in any event."

"Silence!" The order was issued in a loud voice by the queen. She also rose to stand beside her minister. The look she sent Ben was terrible in its ferocity. Nothing of the coy girl remained in her visage. "You killed my betrothed for some nefarious reason. I don't understand what you expected to gain."

"He intended to entangle me in it somehow, Your Majesty," Magnus interjected.

That's when Ben became sure that the Far Isle envoy was behind all of it—or was at least one of the perpetrators. "I can only repeat that I did not kill him." He waved his hand down the front of his clothes.

"Anyone stabbing someone like that would have blood on them. I do not."

"You returned to your room to change clothes," Master Prime Minister retorted.

"Past a dozen guards who didn't notice?" He could see by their expressions that logic wasn't going to sway them.

"Magnus has changed his tunic," Kexen murmured for Ben alone.

The queen lifted her chin. "It matters not what you say. We will get the truth out of you. Take him to the dungeons."

"No!" Kexen grabbed Ben's arm.

He pried it loose as the soldiers descended on him. "Do not get between me and my fate, darling. It's a fight you cannot win, and worrying about you will not help me." The soldiers grabbed his other arm and pulled him into their midst.

"Confine Lady Tentrees to their suite and keep their servants in their own rooms as well. I will not have treacherous people roaming my palace."

Now one of the soldiers had Kexen by both of his arms, dragging him away. Ben's gaze locked with Kexen's for a brief moment, but he saw in his wife's eyes comfort that he wasn't going to resist. There was something else there, as well. Ben couldn't quite read it. It didn't matter. They were taken away surrounded by soldiers and no chance to do more than keep themselves upright and face their fates with as much strength as they could muster. As he got hauled down into the deep recesses of the palace, he could only hope to somehow convince the Iron Shore queen of his innocence. If not, his life would be forfeit. Worse, Kexen's life might also be in jeopardy, and Ben had to do everything in his power and more to protect his wife.

* * * *

"I did *not* kill Rupert."

"Liar!" Master Jailer slapped the crop against Ben's bare chest with as much power as the man's beefy arm could deliver.

Ben cried out, mostly because that seemed to please the men around him, including Master Prime Minister, who watched the proceedings with detached approval. It was impossible to say how long he'd been forced to stand with his arms manacled to the poles he stood between. His shoulders ached and he'd lost track of the number of times he'd been asked the same question with the same punishment when he'd answered honestly but apparently not convincingly. Likely no words or tone of voice would make any difference. The men's minds had been made up already. No other method of extracting the 'truth' had been used, either, surprisingly. He would have expected them to escalate to something more painful — a whip, hot tongs, pulling out his nails, perhaps. The whole ordeal had gone from terrifying to rather boring, and if he weren't worried about how Kexen was faring, he might have been tempted to laugh at his torturers.

Master Jailer got into Ben's face. "You will tell us of your plan!" The way the man huffed with sweat dripping down his temples, one would have thought he was the one being tormented.

Ben almost said '*Or what?*' But there was nothing to be gained by baiting them, so he went with his usual.

"I did not have a plan because I did *not* kill Prince Rupert."

Master Jailer's face reddened. He stepped back and raised his arm once more.

Master Prime Minister intervened. "Enough. This is getting us nowhere. Take him down and throw him in a cell. Time spent with the unpleasant results of his perfidy shall loosen his tongue. If not, we shall begin anew."

Ben winced in real pain as his arms were released, and the guards were rough in taking him to a nearby cell and tossing him onto the filthy rushes. When the door was shut, only a small bit of light showed through the barred window that allowed the guards to see him. The opening was too small to crawl through, even if he could have yanked out the bars, and there was nothing but solid stone walls all around him. It was quite cold, and as there was no blanket, he lay down and piled the pieces of straw over him to provide some warmth. He knew he should sleep but doubted he would. It wasn't the relatively minor pain that kept him awake. It was his worry about his wife. When the queen had sent the boy back to their rooms, it had been a relief. There was nothing to say that he couldn't be harmed there, however. That was especially true, given that he didn't have Baldrick and Euphemia to look out for him. And even though his wife had proved to be able to take care of himself, it was impossible for Ben not to fret.

"Kexen, stay safe," he whispered into the darkness.

Chapter Ten

Kexen had started shredding his dresses the moment the guards had shoved him into his suite. The idiots hadn't even bothered to search for weapons — one of the benefits, he supposed, of being underestimated. All anyone here saw was Ben's pretty wife. They didn't understand that he was that and more. Lady Tentrees might not carry weapons, but Kexen of the Outer Vale did. He'd packed away three short knives and a long one with his set of male attire, just in case. And now that 'in case' situation had arrived. He'd started formulating how he was going to rescue Ben the moment they'd dragged him away.

The first order of business was that he had to free himself, and there was only one way out of the locked and guarded rooms he occupied. The drop from his window was very high, given that they were on the fourth floor of the palace. His only choice was to make a rope, secure it with a piece of furniture and climb down. What he would do after that was still something he was turning over in his mind as he cut his gowns into strips and braided them together. It was a pity to destroy such beauty, but silk was stronger than any other fabric, and the last thing he needed was for his rope to break as he descended. Besides, although no one was going to look in his wardrobe, someone had already invaded his personal rooms to leave him breakfast. If they bothered to look and saw the bedding gone, his plan would be ruined.

When his vision started to blur, he hid the rope away and went to lie down on the settee. He hadn't slept all night but didn't like the idea of being boxed into the bedroom. With his project nearly done and his having to wait until dark to make his escape anyway, he recognized the foolishness of not resting. He wouldn't do Ben any good if he was too tired to think straight. Plus, he had to be prepared to fight—literally. His movements needed to be as sharp as he could make them, and that included putting food into his body. The meal he'd been served was tempting, but he didn't trust that it wasn't drugged or poisoned. He made do with some dried fruit that Euphemia had set out the day before. Gods, he had to free her and her brother as well. *Can I do it? Am I capable?* Foolish questions. He *had* to do this. There was no other place that help would come from. And he knew that there was a plot behind all this that guaranteed Ben would never be able to convince Queen Amira of his innocence.

Kexen awoke sometime later with a start at the sound of the door opening. Gathering the sides of his dressing gown closed, he sat up. A moment later, he felt relief when Minna walked in with a satchel slung over her shoulders and went straight to him. She took his hands and propelled him up and into the bedroom. She shut the door to the sitting room closed. "Forgive the abruptness of my entry, dear friend. How are you?" she added with a concerned look.

"I am well, as you can see. I don't think I need any of your medicine." He was careful with his words, remembering Ben's admonishment about being cautious with his trust.

"I am not here as Madam Apothecary but as your friend." Taking the bag off her shoulder, she went over to the bed, then started removing items. "I brought you bread, dried meat and cheese. I expect you are hungry but suspicious of what might be in the meals they give you. While I have no knowledge that you are right to be so, there is no point in taking chances. Anyone who dares to murder royalty is capable of anything." She held up the food. "And you have no reason to trust me completely, so, as you can see, these aren't adulterated."

"Oh, Minna, I would never think such a thing of you." He realized he meant what he'd said. He hadn't become so jaded already that he couldn't see the good in someone. "Thank you," he added as he took the piece of bread, placed a slice of cheese and meat on top of it and bit off a chunk. "I was worried that I'd have to survive on dried fruit," he said around his mouthful, too hungry to worry about propriety.

Minna shook her head. "I was never going to allow that. There's enough here to last you through the evening, until you make your escape."

Kexen froze in mid-bite. "Sorry?" he said, then swallowed hard.

"I don't expect you to simply sit here until they kill your husband and do gods' know what with you. And I believe I know you well enough to expect that you don't intend to." She got up and paced the room. "The only way out is through the window and down the wall. I have made many friends, which is why the guards let me in, but I don't have the power to convince them to turn a blind eye to your walking out of here. You will have to climb down."

Kexen took another bite and nudged the satchel. "I don't suppose there's rope in here?"

"Sorry. The guards would be suspicious if I carried anything too big. I can't be that obvious and risk being barred altogether." She scanned the room. "You are using the silk of your dresses, I assume?"

"You seem to know an awful lot about escaping locked rooms, Madam Apothecary."

Minna merely grinned. "When your parents start talking about your marrying a girl in the village, you spend a lot of time imagining all the ways you can flee your fate." Her face grew somber. "You can trust me, Kexen. I am your friend, and I'm going to help you and your husband leave the Iron Shore before it's too late."

"And our servants," Kexen intoned, believing now that he could depend on this woman's help.

She nodded. "Yes, of course. It should be fairly easy for me to free them. They aren't under guard the way you are, because no one expects servants to stick their neck out too far for their masters and mistresses. I'll release them and lead them to the spot where we shall meet up after you liberate Lord Tentrees from the dungeon."

"I *will* get him out," Kexen vowed. "But how are we to return to Moorcondia? Until the sea unfreezes, we are trapped here."

Minna walked back to him slowly, a sly grin on her face. "No, you're not. That is what they tell people, but there is a pathway through the mountains that will lead you to Shadow Valley. From there, you can continue overland to Moorcondia. It's not an easy journey in winter, but it's your only hope."

"How do you know of this?"

"Because that is the place I am from, where my dear Vancel found me before bringing me back here. It's an old trade route, made less useful with the increase in sturdy ships. Four people on foot with light packs can make the journey in a few days."

"Amira's soldiers will be hot on our heels, though."

"Hopefully not. Few people remember the trail exists. I'm counting on there being confusion about where you are before anyone can even think of it. And," she added with a deep breath, "I will cover your tracks as much as I can."

Kexen sprang from the bed and grabbed Minna by the hands. "I would be lost without you. Please come with us. I don't want you to be punished for this."

Minna pulled him into a hug. "My dearest Kexen, this is my home now. I want to be buried here next to my Vancel. Please don't worry about me. I have many friends, as I've said, and there is no one better at keeping the queen and her court healthy. I'll be fine." She pulled away again. "Now, let me help you with that rope, and we can finalize the details of our plan as we go."

* * * *

Kexen used his teeth to tug on his second glove. It was a tight fit, but that was needed in order to hold onto the rope properly. He caught sight of himself in the vanity mirror. Gone was Lady Tentrees, replaced with the Outer Vale boy that he'd been raised as. He was equally comfortable in this mode of dress, although he'd spent so much time in women's clothing that it felt and looked a little odd. No matter, this was what he needed to free Ben and make their escape. His tight leather trousers, thick tunic covered by a woolen jacket and sturdy fur-lined boots would keep him warm and sufficiently agile to climb, run and fight as needed. There was no elaborate hairstyle, only a tight braid tucked into the back of his shirt.

Wrapped around his waist was a pouch used by travelers to hide valuables. He was glad to have thought of it. In it he'd secured some coin and his jewelry. It wasn't merely sentiment that caused him to bring the beautiful pieces that Ben and the duchess had gifted him with. They might be needed for bargaining their way back home. For more immediate needs, he'd tucked a blade into each boot and at the small of his back. The long knife looped into his belt would give him a fighting chance of reaching Ben, should anyone confront him. He flew his hand to that weapon when he heard the outer door open. He relaxed when Minna came through the doorway to the bedroom.

She looked him up and down. "My, this is a different look for you, Lady Tentrees."

"Yes, but this is me just as much as my gowns were."

"And a good thing, too, for your husband's sake."

Alarm shot through him. "Have you heard anything about how he is?"

"Only that he is alive."

Kexen grimaced. "That's the best we can hope for at the moment. I'll free him shortly and carry him on my back if I have to."

"Let's hope it doesn't come to that." Minna opened her satchel on the bed. She tossed food aside and reached into the depths to pull out what appeared to be two small glass vials containing colored liquid and bound together by a string. She handed them over to Kexen, along with a small leather sack. "Put these carefully in the pouch and tie it to your belt in the back."

Kexen did as told. "What are they?"

"Right now, nothing of note. When the liquids mix, however, they create a gas that will knock out anyone who breathes it in. Be careful not to let them bump against the wall as you climb and make sure to reposition them once you're on the ground so that you can grab them quickly when you need them."

"This is how I will free Ben without having to fight whoever guards him."

"Exactly. There is an anteroom at the bottom of the curved stairs to the dungeon. That's where the guards spend their time during their shift. You have to throw the vials on the ground to smash them, cover your face and wait for the cloud to dissipate before continuing. It happens rapidly, so you shouldn't be affected by it yourself."

Kexen gave into the impulse to hug the woman and kiss her cheek. "I couldn't do this without you."

"Oh, you would have found a way, I have no doubt. But time is wasting. The after-supper revelries are subdued tonight, given the period of mourning, but everyone is there, nevertheless. It's your best chance to descend without being seen."

"I know. I'm ready."

"Do you need to go over the map once more?"

"No." Kexen tapped the side of his head. "It's securely here."

With Minna's help, he tied one end of the rope to the leg of the table in the sitting room, then threw open the window and looked down. Seeing no one, he lowered the rest of the rope and was pleased to see it reached nearly to the ground. *Thank the gods and Ben that I had such an extensive trousseau.* There was nothing else to do but get on with it. He wanted to say more to his friend. They'd had so little time together. But every second meant Ben's life could be taken before he reached him. Slinging his leg over the window ledge, he grabbed the rope and began his descent with his feet braced against the palace's stone wall.

It was slow going because the alternative was to drop to his likely death. So he took his time and was glad that he had climbed rocks at home for fun. Heights didn't bother him, either, and his muscles were sufficiently strong to keep his descent under control. Still, they shook a little from the strain by the time he was able to jump the short distance that was left. He took a moment to catch his breath and watched as Minna pulled the rope back up. That had been her idea, too. There would be nothing for anyone to find now that he was free. And to that point, he dashed to the nearby bushes in order to make his way unseen around the palace grounds. His walk that first full day after arriving had given him a good sense of the palace's design. He knew what to avoid as the more populated areas, including the sentries. Minna's quickly drawn map had been critical to show him the best door to enter to make his way to the dungeon with the fewest number of steps—and hopefully unseen. He pictured it now as he slunk through the shrubbery.

Hang on, Ben. I'm coming for you.

* * * *

Ben shifted gingerly to lean against one cold wall. It actually felt good on his back, the latest recipient of his jailer's lackluster interrogation. He was hungry and miserable, too. Worse, though, was his continued worry about Kexen. He dared not ask anyone about his wife. No one would care to tell him, and it would only call attention to a weak spot in him. These relatively mild beatings were nothing against his resolve, but if they laid even one stripe across Kexen's delicate skin, Ben would lose his shit. He might be convinced to tell any lie they wanted to hear to spare his precious love such treatment.

Yes, he'd finally gone there. The word 'love' had been rattling around his bored brain since his imprisonment. To deny it seemed ridiculous under the circumstances, particularly as he'd only be trying to convince himself. If his life was coming to an end, the least he could do was face his feelings honestly. His real regret was that he'd likely never have the chance to tell his wife. Kexen had deserved better than what he'd gotten from Ben, from the rushed courtship to the brutal wedding night — and now captivity in a foreign land. If they somehow managed to get out of this mess, he vowed to never subject his wife to another diplomatic mission. They would make a quiet life together wherever Kexen wanted. With his eyes closed, Ben let the fantasy take him away.

The sound of glass breaking, then muttered oaths and finally a loud crash pulled Ben from his reverie. He jumped to his feet and put his face against the barred window. There was little to see as there appeared to be some kind of fog inside the entrance to the dungeon.

He shook his head, sure that it was his vision that was fuzzy. But no, that was truly smoke of some kind that was also quickly dissipating. A hand and the uniformed arm it was attached to lay on the floor just visible in his line of sight. It was obviously a guard's, but what had knocked the man to the ground? He got his answer in the next instant when a familiar form appeared and walked toward him. It was his wife, although not in the manner he'd become accustomed to seeing him. This young man was dressed for fighting, with a knife at his belt and an armful of weapons that must have been stripped from the guards. The cloth covering his nose and mouth did nothing to hide his identity, either—not for Ben, anyway. His heart did a slow roll at the sight, and tears pricked at his eyes. He hadn't fully appreciated how terrified he'd been about Kexen's situation. He seemed in fine form.

Kexen raced to Ben's door and dumped the weaponry while uncovering his face. "Ben! Thank the gods. Stand back while I figure out which of these keys will unlock the door." He held up a large ring filled with them. Because Ben had no way of helping with the decision, he took a step back and took the time he had to bring his emotions under control. His wife needed him to be strong. Being freed from the cell was only the first step on a long road. They would have to find somewhere to hide for the rest of the winter. In the thickness of the woods, probably, or there might be hidden caves at the base of the mountains. It wouldn't be easy to survive and stay out of sight of those who would hound them. Then when spring came, there was the problem of stowing aboard a ship… No, he couldn't get ahead of himself. One step at a time.

"Got it." The door swung open and Kexen stood staring at him, his gaze raking Ben's body. "How badly are you hurt? Can you walk or should I carry you?"

Ben nearly laughed at the idea of his wife shouldering his heavy weight as they made their escape. He would crawl first. The fearful expression on Kexen's face stayed Ben's response. He needed to erase that look and comfort the boy. "I am passably well, my darling. These people are terrible at torture."

"Don't joke about such a thing!"

"I'm sorry, but it's true." He went to him and took hold of him by his shoulders. "I'm hungry, cold and a bit sore. That's all. And I'm sure I smell awful," he added with a smile to show that he wasn't being merely stoic.

Kexen grabbed him in a quick, light hug. "I don't care about that. I'm just glad you're not as hurt as I'd pictured."

Ignoring the sting of pain caused by the contact, Ben tightened the hold. "I worried about you, too. My imagination ran wild. I honestly feared they would bring you down here to loosen my tongue. Thank the gods that I overestimated their cunning. Or maybe it's all simply theater to whoever is behind this and not meant to do anything other than keep us out of the way."

Kexen pulled back. "I have my suspicions about that."

"As do I. First we must make haste and find somewhere to lie low until we form a plan." He followed his wife out of the cell.

"It's already set. We have a way out of the Iron Shore, thanks to Minna." Kexen scooped to pick up the weapons again. "You need warmer clothes. This guard looks about your size. I'm sure he won't mind lending you some." Kexen had already put his armful of stolen weaponry back on the floor and out of reach of the unconscious guards. For a personal groomer, Ben's wife surely had been trained in warfare at some point. He knew just what to do. His estimation of the boy kept going up. And he was kneeling on the floor to tug off the man's boots.

Grabbing a piece of bread and meat that must have been left over from the guards' dinner, Ben started to help. He shoved the food into his mouth as he did so. "How did you knock them out?"

"Oh, Ben, take some time to chew properly. I don't want you to choke. But to answer your question, Minna gave me those shattered vials over there. When I threw them on the floor, they broke, the liquids mixed and they created a gas that caused these men to pass out."

Ben paused halfway through putting a scratchy woolen shirt on himself. "That's why your face was covered. Are we at risk from succumbing ourselves?"

"No. It's fast-acting. We're fine. Here... Let me help."

Between the two of them, they managed to outfit Ben for his escape. Feeling the need for urgency, he didn't bother with more than was necessary, and that included taking a sword and a few knives for himself. He was not a soldier, but he knew how to fight and with protecting his wife as a keen incentive, he was prepared to slaughter anyone in the palace who got in their way. Kexen also grabbed a sword, although he chose a shorter one, a better fit for his size.

"I trust you can use that, darling?"

Kexen gave him a fierce look. "I can, and I will." With that, he tossed the weaponry they didn't take into

Ben's cell, then locked the door. He pushed the key ring through the bars for good measure. "There, that's at least some comfort. When they wake up, they'll have to go to the armory to re-arm themselves. Every moment of delay can only help us."

Ben grabbed his arm as he tried to pass. "You are very clever, wife. I love you even more for all this." Kexen's eyes went wide. "Yes, I just confessed that I love you. I wanted to make sure you knew before we face whatever is out there for us." It hadn't been planned, yet now that the words were out, he was glad he'd spoken them. While he hoped they would survive their flight, there was a strong likelihood that they would not.

No fool he, Kexen frowned. "Don't tell me that just because you think we're about to die."

Ben dared to give his wife a quick kiss. "It is the truth, regardless of the reason I'm blurting it out. Now, we must flee, and you will stay *behind* me. In this I will brook no argument."

"You don't know where we're headed."

"I'm sure you can instruct me as we go along."

Not giving his wife any more time to argue the point, Ben started up the stairs. He went as slowly and quietly as he could manage, taking a brief moment to appreciate that Kexen was even better at making no sound. At each turn of the twisting steps, he expected to be confronted by someone. Surely it couldn't be this easy for him to be broken out of his prison. There was nothing, though, to stop them, and when they reached the landing, they were able to slip past the two guards standing at a distance with their backs to them. With silent commands, Kexen led him down what had to be a service corridor. The security of the palace was poorly laid out, in his opinion—too focused on the areas that the important residents frequented and not on plugging every hole. Not that he was complaining... Anything that aided their escape was fine by him. The purpose of the hallway was confirmed when they came upon an open door to a room that buzzed with chatter.

Kexen pulled him up short and urged Ben to plaster himself against the wall. The boy slinked to the doorway and peeked around it before dashing past. He looked again from the other side before beckoning Ben to come. Good thing that the servants were so loud, because Ben was not quite as quiet in his movements. He made it though, and there was no hue or cry, so they hadn't been seen. They continued on their way until reaching an outside door. It opened with ease and there were footsteps in the snow that Ben could only assume belonged to his wife.

When they were far enough away from the palace to be heard, he whispered in Kexen's ear. "How did you escape our suite?"

"I made a rope out of my dresses and climbed down the window." The boy said this as if it were both obvious and no great accomplishment.

"That's four stories!" Ben couldn't bear thinking of his wife dangling so high up.

"Indeed, it took my entire wardrobe to make a rope long enough." Kexen seemed unimpressed with his own feat.

"Astounding."

"It was nothing. Come this way."

They sprinted through the palace gardens to the far most corner of the cultivated land. This inner courtyard of the palace was likewise under-guarded. Then there was a narrow door set inside the stone wall behind a large bush. One had to know it was there to find it, and of course, the information must have come from Minna. It opened easily and Ben felt elated and relieved when he spied Baldrick, Euphemia and Madam Apothecary standing just inside the tree line of the forest. But his hopes were dashed in the next instant when their expressions registered. He tried to grab Kexen before it was too late and failed. Not that it would have mattered because they were quickly hemmed in by three soldiers who came upon them from the rear. By the time Kexen had skidded to a stop, Master Prime Minister and Magnus, with two more guards flanking Minna and the servants, had already emerged from the shadows to stand triumphantly.

Ben turned so that he could keep all seven of his foes within his line of sight and did his best to put Kexen behind him. "Well, it is somewhat gratifying to learn that my theory was correct."

"I'm sorry," Minna cried out. "I didn't know they were following me."

Master Prime Minister sneered at her. "You forget, Madam Apothecary, that I have eyes and ears everywhere. Nothing happens in this palace that I don't know about."

Ben felt Kexen stirring behind him, and he tried to keep him quiet as he spoke. The longer he could keep these men talking, the better chance he had of mounting an attack. "Including no doubt that the queen's betrothed was going to be assassinated. By Magnus, I assume? Who else would Rupert have allowed to get so close to him? Unless it was you, Master Prime Minister?" He shook his head. "No, you're not one to get his hands dirty, are you? And as my wife observed at the time, Magnus had changed his tunic. It wouldn't do to try to dazzle the queen on the dance floor with her betrothed's blood being smeared on her dress."

Magnus took a step forward. "Yes, yes, how very clever of you, Tentrees, to figure it out." He looked at Master Prime Minister. "Why are we waiting? I'm freezing my balls off out here. Kill them and be done with it."

Again, Kexen shifted behind him. Ben kept talking to keep attention on himself, even as he tried once more to keep his wife still by shifting his body. "Yes, do. Magnus needs to start wooing Queen Amira in earnest without interference. She's too vibrant to mourn for long, and when she is sufficiently enamored with your dick, you can oh so casually work in how you are descended from Iron Shore royalty." He *tsk*ed. "It wasn't merely average people who struck out for new land. Lesser members of the royal family were undoubtedly seeking a place of their own to rule. It must have been quite irksome to some of their descendants when the native population of Far Isle managed to convince your ancestors to give up a good deal of their power."

Magnus' emotions betrayed him. His face screwed up with fury. "I am a *prince*. I should not have to be ordered and judged by those grubby peasants. Here I shall rule by right of birth and answer to no one."

"Except the queen." Ben shook his head. "Oh, but of course she'll be gone, too. A hunting accident, no doubt, after you are married. That seems to be the handiest way of getting rid of someone. The dense forest hides secrets very well. She'll be struck down early at the will of the gods…just like her father." He stared directly at the minister.

"You are clever, Tentrees. And you only really became an integral part of our plan when we saw your *unusual* wife. Exactly Rupert's taste. After that it was a matter of putting you out of commission—but not too much so. Rupert was terribly predictable and gave you the perfect motive to kill him.

"Alas, I had really intended to keep you and your wife locked up until the spring. We didn't want to kill you or give Moorcondia an excuse to wage war. We would have magnanimously agreed to return their murderer to them. Your escape has given me no choice."

"Maybe if you'd let me in on the plan, I would have stayed rotting in your dungeon."

Whatever Magnus or the minister might have said as a retort was cut off by Kexen making his move. Before Ben even realized what his wife was doing, there was a thud and a muted cry as one of the soldiers who had come up behind them fell to the ground with a knife sticking out of his chest. While the others hesitated, Ben drew his stolen sword out of his equally stolen belt and charged the soldier who was starting to kneel by his fallen comrade. He felt without seeing Kexen moving in the other direction and out of the corner of his eye, he saw Baldrick and Euphemia make their own moves. Even Minna sprang into action, attacking the minister.

Then there was chaos.

Chapter Eleven

Kexen concentrated on the man he attacked, trusting that Ben could take care of himself. It was hard to let go, especially as he'd seen the violence visited upon his husband's body. Ben had laughed it off as nothing, and while it was true that far worse could have been done, those wounds had to hurt. Plus, Ben had been underfed and was likely weaker than he let on. A fight against a man who suffered from none of those impediments was going to be a difficult one to win. Still, there was no choice. Even with Minna and the servants joining the fray with whatever pieces of wood were at hand, they were fighting well-armed soldiers, and nothing was to say that more weren't within shouting distance.

He'd been wise to pick up the short sword. While its reach wasn't as long as his opponent's, Kexen was able to wield it without a struggle. And he was skilled. It had been ages since he'd practiced fighting, but his body remembered the moves without prompting. He thrusted and parried around the clearing, trying to take the fight away from the others. They stood a better chance of success if each battle could be fought without entanglement. Plus, he didn't want Ben distracted by worry that Kexen needed help. Perhaps it had been a mistake to dress solely as a woman — and a pampered one at that. His husband had never truly had the chance to see the whole of him and to appreciate his strengths.

I love you. No, he couldn't allow himself to be distracted by that memory — nor would he dwell now on how he should have said the words back. He knew that he loved Ben and had assumed he would be the first to say it. Maybe the only one. But Ben had beaten him to it. *Why didn't I tell him what's in my heart?* There had been shock at the sudden declaration, yes, and an urgent need not to dawdle. And yet, it would have taken so little time. He wanted to shout the words now but didn't. Ben needed to keep all his concentration on staying alive. Besides, he didn't want to bare his soul to the vicious people who had conspired against them and were now trying to kill them. Nor did he want them to think he said those words because he believed he would have no other chance. Fighting required mental strength as well as physical. It wouldn't do to show any sign of weakness.

His arm was tiring, though. Agility was his greatest skill when it came to sword play, not raw power. And his opponent had both a height and muscular advantage over him. Each time the man delivered a blow against Kexen's blade, he felt the jarring through his bones. He couldn't keep up the fight for much longer. So he took the chance of stepping closer and when the soldier brought his weapon down again, Kexen was driven to his knees with the force of their swords clashing. But it was a controlled fall, putting him where he wanted to be. As vulnerable as he was in that position, it gave him a chance to pull the knife from one of his boots and thrust it into the man's groin. He'd known he'd have only the one chance, to stick his opponent in the vulnerable place between the padding of the man's uniform. The moment he felt the hilt could go no farther, he rolled away, before springing back to his feet.

Kexen stood staring, taking great gulps of air, his lungs burning and his muscles screaming from the fight. The soldier swayed before him with wide eyes before collapsing. Blood spurted from his wound, a sure sign that Kexen had hit the artery he'd been aiming for. He knew no satisfaction from what he'd just done. Taking another's life was not something he'd ever done, yet as necessary as it had been, he pushed aside any guilt over it. There was still a battle being waged. His first instinct was to help Ben, but his husband could take care of himself. The more vulnerable people were Minna and the servants—or so he'd thought. As he sprinted to help them, he realized he wasn't needed. Minna had the minister flat on the ground, her knee in the small of his back and his hair wrapped in her fist. He was going nowhere and howled in impotent rage. Euphemia delivered a skull-crushing blow to the soldier she fought with, while her brother held the other one in a chokehold until the man slumped to the ground.

Kexen trained his eye on Magnus, who stood apart from the fray. The man gave him a baiting grin as he held up his hands to show he was unarmed. *Coward.* Apparently he didn't want the throne badly enough to spill his own blood over it—not that Kexen trusted that the man wasn't a threat. He'd killed Rupert, after all. Kexen kept him in his line of sight while checking on

Ben's situation. His husband thrust his sword into the chest of his adversary, bringing him down as he pulled it out again. Then Ben looked around, and as soon as his gaze landed on Kexen, there was a clear expression of relief. He smiled at him, sending a feeling of warmth through Kexen. He could see pride and adoration in his husband's face. Once more, Kexen wanted to shout his love, but matters were not settled yet.

"Madam Apothecary," Ben called out, "I believe it's safe to let the minister up at this point. He appears unarmed."

Minna yanked hard on the hair before replying. "He is. I've searched him already." The woman jumped off the man and went beyond his reach.

Master Prime Minister got up slowly and staggered closer to Magnus. "This isn't over, Tentrees. I'll see your head cleaved from your shoulders. All of you will die," he added with a sneer.

Ben surveyed the area around them. "I see no cohorts racing to your rescue. And I think it is your life that is forfeit for what you have done. Queen Amira doesn't strike me as someone willing to forgive such treachery."

The minister merely barked out a laugh and Magnus put his hands behind his back to stand in a relaxed manner. He didn't look worried at all, and that was troubling. "You think the queen will listen to you over me?" the minister spit out. "You're escaped prisoners and a traitorous foreigner who never should have been trusted in the first place." He shot a look of pure hatred at Minna. "The most you've gained is a head start. The queen will never believe you."

"She will me." Madam Chamberlain stepped out from the doorway in the stone wall.

Ben shifted, probably so that he could see her and react if she made a threatening move. It seemed unlikely that the stately older woman would do so, but then Kexen would never have expected Minna or the servants to be such fierce fighters, either. It didn't do to make assumptions, and the woman's presence was an odd turn of events. *Let's hope she's on our side.*

"Madam Chamberlain," the minister sputtered. "What are you doing here? Surely you didn't help these villains escape?"

"Spare me your theatrics, Master Prime Minister. I heard everything and know where the guilt lies." She spoke directly to Ben now. "I knew that you were innocent of Prince Rupert's murder. One of my servants saw an Iron Shore man do the deed and was petrified of saying anything publicly." Her gaze shifted to Magnus. "He made an understandable mistake. Now, I know it was you he saw."

Madam Chamberlain walked closer to Ben, a sign that she trusted him. "I was biding my time to bring the matter to the queen without putting myself or the servant in danger. I apologize for that. I can see now that matters were more urgent than I had understood. Fortunately, I caught sight of you going past the scullery and followed you."

Ben gave a respectful nod. "I thank the gods that my stealth and speed were lacking in this case."

Kexen felt some measure of relief. While he believed the woman when she'd said she had the ear of the queen, he couldn't truly relax until Magnus and the minister were locked down in the dank cells where Ben had been kept. He also wasn't entirely sure they could trust Amira, no matter what the facts were. "What do we do now?" He'd asked the question generally but his focus was on his husband.

Before Ben could respond, Madam Chamberlain pursed her lips and issued a series of variously toned whistles. "I've just called to some of my house guards. They are loyal to me," she added, obviously astute enough to understand their concerns.

"Then it's over." Kexen let out a slow breath of relief.

A movement caught his attention. Magnus' right arm was twitching ever so minutely. Kexen recognized the movement because he'd done the same not long ago as he'd reached for the knife he'd hidden in the back of his waistband. Time seemed to slow. Kexen screamed, "He has a knife!" before lunging toward the man.

Even as he tried to stop Magnus, he could see that he was too late. The knife was leaving the man's hand and its trajectory was clear. Kexen pivoted and threw himself into its path. The impact was hardly noticeable, but he went tumbling to the ground, nevertheless. His sword flew from his hand at the jarring impact, and he was tossed onto his back. Although the wind was knocked out of him, he otherwise felt no pain. He thought perhaps he hadn't been hit after all. But when he tried to lift his head, the world spun and there was a sharp prick on one side. That's when he saw the knife hilt sticking up from his abdomen. He dropped his head back and stared up at the night sky. It was really quite beautiful.

There was a battle cry the likes of which he'd never heard before. Someone ran by him. *No, not someone. Ben.* Footsteps shook the ground. There was a masculine scream, more of rage than fear by the sound of it. Then there was silence for a few moments before there was a flurry of movement and the sound of what seemed like a million voices. Kexen tried again to sit up, worried about his husband and not certain that there weren't more battles to be fought.

Minna dropped down beside him, putting her hand to his forehead to gently keep him in place. "Easy, dear boy. There is nothing to worry about. Madam Chamberlain speaks the truth about her loyal guards, and everyone is safe…your husband included."

Kexen went still and concentrated on taking one breath after the other as the pain morphed into something hideous. "Is Ben hurt?"

"I'm well, my darling." Ben's face appeared within Kexen's field of vision as he sat on his other side and took his hand. "Please do as Madam Apothecary advises. You have been magnificent in all of this, but now it's time for you to be cared for."

Minna prodded the area around the knife. "This is good. The precious items you hid around your middle helped to keep the knife from piercing too far in."

Despite her comforting words, her touch made Kexen scream inside. He clamped his lips tightly, determined not to cause Ben any more worry. "Hmm-m," was all he could say in response.

"If it makes you feel better," Minna added, "someone is going to have to crawl under a thorn bush to recover Magnus' head. It was no more than he deserved. And this needs to come out," she added.

Ben squeezed his hand. "Look at me, Kexen. Keep your eyes on me."

Kexen obeyed, and happily so. All the strength had drained out of him, and he simply didn't want to have to think about anything. He'd always thought Ben's eyes were merely brown. As he gazed into them this closely, he could see that there was amber swirled within the iris. *Lovely*. That was his last thought before obscene pain finally forced a scream out of him and sent the world into black.

* * * *

"Here. If you're not going to eat, you need to drink this. You'll do the boy no good if you collapse from lack of nutrition."

Ben took the offered mug and sipped at the warm drink, not caring what it tasted like. He kept his gaze on his wife, as he'd been doing for days, clasping his hand so that he knew he wasn't alone. Minna had said that people often were aware of their surroundings, even when unconscious. If his presence helped Kexen even in a small way to recover, he wanted to be there.

He ran his thumb along his wife's palm. "He seems cooler today, don't you think?"

Minna moved to the other side of the bed and placed the back of her hand against Kexen's forehead. "Yes, he does. I think his fever has final broken for the last time."

Their hopes had been raised and dashed a few times over the days as Kexen's fever had come and gone. Thank the gods for Minna. It was clear to Ben that without the woman's formidable skills, Kexen would not have survived his wound. While it hadn't been deep, infection had set in. Minna had suspected that it had been deliberately laced with something to cause that very problem. It made Ben want to resurrect that fucker, Magnus, so that he could kill him all over again.

Minna had opened up her home to them, as well. She'd offered it unprompted that terrible night when she'd pulled the knife out and bound Kexen's torso as best she could. Somehow she'd sensed that Ben didn't want to return to the heart of Amira's palace. Although Madam Chamberlain had so far proved steadfast, it still felt as if danger lurked all around them. She and the queen were rooting out those loyal to Master Prime Minister, but Ben preferred being in this secluded spot with Minna, Baldrick and Euphemia playing guards as well as helpmates.

"I can never repay you for what you've done." He tore his gaze from his wife's face to look at Minna. "I owe you for Kexen's life."

"We are friends, Lord Tentrees. You owe me nothing." With that, she quietly left the room.

"She's right."

Ben nearly jumped out of his chair before leaning over his wife's face. "My love?"

Kexen's eyes fluttered halfway open. "I am parched."

Elated, Ben jumped to his feet, reluctant to let go of his wife's hand but needing both of his to pour a cup of water, then hold Kexen's head up in order for him to drink. "Take small sips. Minna and I have been feeding you liquids in tiny drops on your tongue." The order hadn't been necessary because Kexen didn't have the strength to do more than that, anyway. He sighed and closed his eyes as he sank his head back into the pillow.

Putting the cup down, Ben said, "I'll get Minna."

"No." Kexen made an aborted attempt to grab Ben's hand. "I want just you for now."

Torn between worry and wanting to give his wife whatever he desired, Ben sat in his seat and clasped Kexen's hand between his own. "I am here for you, my darling."

"Where…?"

"We're in Minna's house, safe. And before you tax your strength with more questions, I'll tell you that Madam Chamberlain was as good as her word. Master Prime Minister and those loyal to him are rotting in the dungeon until the queen decides their fate."

A smile played on Kexen's lips. "Good."

Ben kissed his hand, wanting to do more, yet terrified he'd make his wife's health worse. "You saved my life, darling. Don't do something like that ever again. No fate is worse than fearing that you are gone. I love you." He'd said the words before in haste. It was important for his wife to know that he meant them.

Opening his eyes again, Kexen glared at him as much as his wan visage and depleted energy could. "Stop doing that." His tone was no less fierce for the words being uttered in a near whisper.

Ben's heart sank. It hadn't occurred to him that his wife wouldn't want to hear the sentiment. He'd misjudged Kexen again. The boy's fun-loving demeanor and appreciation for pretty clothes had led Ben to believe that Kexen wanted a relationship based on love. Maybe he saw their marriage only for what it had started out being—a business arrangement with a little diplomatic excitement mixed in. He opened his words to apologize for pushing the issue.

"Dearest, Ben, for a smart man you can be dumb sometimes."

Ben raised his eyebrows. "My darling, Kexen, please don't tax your strength berating me. We can discuss this later."

"No." Kexen swallowed with obvious difficulty but kept his eyes open and fixed on Ben. "You keep beating me to the punch. Give me a chance to say the words back... I love you, too. And I'll throw myself in front of as many knives heading your way as I please." He managed to scowl before closing his eyes again.

Ben couldn't stop from grinning broadly. It was a pity his wife couldn't see his joy. Then again, it might be better that he not. Ben was feeling far too smug. "You are a marvel, Kexen of the Outer Vale."

"That's Lady Tentrees to you."

Ben laughed, somewhat amazed that he could do so when not so long ago, he'd been terrified that his wife would be taken from him. "My apologies." He sat silently for a while, sure that Kexen had fallen asleep, a far better situation than being rendered unconscious from his wound and fever. He wanted to get Minna but didn't want to alarm his wife, should he wake again and find him gone. It was soothing, too, to simply listen to Kexen's even breathing.

Then Kexen jerked and his eyes flew open again. "I can feel the pain," the boy admitted.

Ben jumped to his feet. "I'll fetch Minna. I'm sure she has a potion to ease you."

Before he could go, Kexen's grip tightened. "I want to go home, Ben."

He reached down to run a soothing hand over his wife's brow. "And so we shall, but we can't risk the overland trip. Minna says it's harsh. You need time to regain your strength, as well. We'll leave when the sea permits it. Don't worry," he added when Kexen frowned. "Minna has something that she swears will keep the seasickness at bay.

"And I'm going to ask the captain to put us into port nearer to Northcliff. We'll visit my family and yours before we settle down in that lovely cottage Prince Soren gifted you with."

"Your career…"

"Means nothing to me, compared to you. We've had enough excitement serving Moorcondia. I'm rather looking forward to a life as a gentleman farmer." He leaned down to plant a chaste kiss on his wife's lips. "I love you, Kexen, and you better get used to my saying that a lot. The first time I saw you, I knew I wanted you in my bed. I never dreamed how you'd capture my heart. We belong to each other, Lady Tentrees, and I will prove that to you every day for the rest of our lives."

Epilogue

"I think summer has finally arrived." Kexen lay with his back against his husband's chest, staring through the open windows of the gazebo. "I think this is going to be my favorite spot in the entire estate," he added.

It was a bold statement, considering that he and Ben were still exploring the 'cottage' that had been given to him, along with the land included and all its outbuildings. He hadn't yet visited with each of his many tenants, either. While he was much recovered from his near-fatal stabbing, his energy often flagged suddenly. Ben was always there, watching for any little sign that he was tired and whisking him back to bed. And that wasn't as fun as it sounded. Their sex life had resumed only in a measured way at Ben's insistence. Blow jobs and hand jobs were all very well, but as each day passed and Kexen's strength returned, his thirst grew to be mounted by his husband.

"It is lovely here," Ben observed. "I appreciate the way the sunshine plays along your hair." So saying, he lifted a few strands and let them sift through his fingers. "I'm very glad Minna didn't have to cut it *all* off."

"It was quite the tangle after so many days fighting a fever." He twisted in his husband's arms and propped his chin on his fist. "I'm all better now, you know."

"Says the man who practically fell asleep into his soup bowl last night."

Kexen rolled his eyes. "Okay, so I get overly tired still. I'm not at the moment, though," he added with a flutter of his lashes.

Ben laughed and cupped Kexen's ass. "Are you fishing for me to take your sweet cock in my mouth, wife?"

"No." Kexen slid to a sitting position. "I want yours inside me."

There was a sudden twinkle in Ben's eyes and a hardness rose up noticeably from his loose trousers. "Alas, my darling, even if you are truly up for such an exercise, we don't have any of Minna's cream with us."

Kexen took great delight in shooting down that objection. "I prepped myself before we came out here." He leaned closer when he added, "I'm positively dripping with anticipation, and this wonderful tingling warmth is infusing my ass. It's giving me all kinds of ideas."

Ben dropped his jaw and expelled a harsh breath. Taking that wordless reaction as a 'yes', Kexen didn't bother with more conversation. His husband may have left the diplomatic corps, but he was always quick to negotiate everything. Kexen was determined not to give him the chance in this case.

He palmed Ben's length through the cloth of his trousers, appreciating the groan he elicited before untying the laces to them and freeing his husband's cock. As always, he was awestruck by it, loving its length and girth. It was warm and hard when he clasped it, the satiny smoothness of the stretched skin interrupted only by the engorged veins on either side of the shaft. A pearl of cum was already beading on the slit, testament to how much his husband wanted him. Kexen licked his lips before opening his mouth as wide as he could and taking the head of Ben's dick inside. Salty bitterness burst on his tongue immediately. Closing his eyes, he moaned. *Delicious.* Given the way Ben jerked at his touch, he knew he was having the right effect.

Ben laid a light hand on top of Kexen's head, not pushing, merely staying there as another point of connection between them. Then he tightened his grip as Kexen sucked and laved the cock with abandon. Kexen knew it would take little effort to make the man come. That would be counterproductive to his goal, however. While Ben was a virile man, Kexen didn't think he could wait for him to recover in order to fuck him properly. So he gripped the base of his shaft as he lavished the rest of it with attention.

"Gods, take me deeper."

Kexen was happy to comply, sucking the cock into his throat. It was impossible to swallow the man completely, the presence of his hand notwithstanding, but he took as much as he could and worked the top half of the dick with his throat muscles. Ben bucked and writhed, digging his fingers into Kexen's scalp. If not for the death grip he had on the man's cock, Kexen would have been choking on his cum for sure. His own dick stood erect, brushing against the skirt of his gown. He'd dressed deliberately this way, with no smallclothes, to avoid as many impediments as possible. He shuddered himself from the rasping of the cloth against his sensitive head and his hole fairly itched with the need to be filled. His sphincter spasmed uncontrollably with anticipation.

When he judged them both to be beyond waiting, he pulled his mouth off Ben's dick but kept fisting the shaft. Hitching his skirt up with his free hand, he wiggled into position. Both he and Ben groaned when the tip of Ben's cock teased the puckered ring. Kexen forced it open slowly, the cream doing its job of making his flesh more pliable. Relaxing was easy, as well, because he now knew the pleasure awaiting him. And the setting was wonderful — warm and gorgeous, their own haven, with no one about to see. Nothing would interfere with his taking his husband's cock into his body. The slight burn of being stretched only added to his arousal. It was nothing like the pain of his wedding night, a distant memory now that he released forever into the wind. And the benefit of the sweet mixture of pleasure and discomfort was a surprising secret of sex.

Kexen shuddered and moaned with his eyes closed as Ben's cock filled him completely. It was heady stuff being in control of all this raw, masculine power. For long moments, he sat there with his face lifted into the sunlight, reveling in being so completely and deliciously filled. It was only when Ben gave some grunt of frustration that he began to ride his husband with long, slow posts of his body. He pressed his palms on Ben's chest for leverage and undulated his hips with each down stroke. The angle helped to increase the rubbing from Ben's dick against his prostate. The sparks that the brushing sent shooting through him caused his breath to hitch. He huffed out small cries as he picked up speed, determined now to bring them both to completion.

Then Ben grabbed him by the waist with one hand to thrust upward as Kexen pushed his ass down, while also reaching under Kexen's skirt to find his cock to jerk it. Now they both raced forward, slamming their bodies together and mingling their moans in the clear summer air. Kexen could barely hang onto Ben as the climax overtook him. He lost all rhythm, writhing uncontrollably while Ben pumped himself inside his quivering channel. Warmth splashed within him as his own cock jumped in Ben's grasp to coat him with cum. Kexen rode the climax with his head tipped back until he collapsed on top of his husband.

They lay there for a long while, sated and with their bodies still joined until Ben's cock softened. Kexen clenched to keep it inside him even so, but Ben gently nudged him over to separate their bodies and hugged Kexen against his side. Everything was perfect, and as sleep started to claim him, he said, "I love you."

He smiled in triumph. Since he'd first woken from his injury, it had become a running contest to see which of them would say the words first at any given time. It was roughly a tie so far, but they had many years ahead of them. He would never get enough of declaring his love for his husband and was sure in the knowledge that Ben wouldn't, either. His dreams had come true. His marriage was a love match after all.

The blaring of a horn in the near distance startled him awake. He looked around, even as Ben brought them to a sitting position. "What was that?" The sound echoed around them again. He slapped his hand against Ben's chest. "That's Prince Soren's herald!"

With this hair mussed and a wild look on his face, Ben said, "They're not due until tomorrow." He scrambled to get them on their feet.

Kexen smoothed his skirts and was dismayed to see an obvious stain where his cum had landed. "We can't greet them like this. Come on." He grabbed Ben's hand to leave the gazebo.

His husband had other ideas. Swooping Kexen into his strong arms, the man dashed down the steps and sprinted toward the house. He was laughing as they went, a more carefree man now that they lived a quiet life. Kexen couldn't help but join in with him. The servants averted their eyes as they raced to the back stairs.

Euphemia met them on the landing. "My lady, the prince and duchess are coming up the drive. They'll be here any moment."

"I know!" Kexen laughed some more. "Don't worry. Lord Tentrees will act as my maid. Make sure the household is ready for our guests."

The woman passed them on the stairs, muttering about propriety. Paying her no mind, Ben raced down the hallway to their large suite. He set Kexen on his feet, then promptly added to their time problem by kissing him senseless. Kexen didn't mind, and knowing the prince and duchess as he did, he doubted they would, either. It was surprising how quickly he and his husband made themselves presentable, because they couldn't stop laughing as they did so. And they helped each other, washing and dressing in the shared space they'd picked to do so together on a daily basis. And as with their illustrious guests, they opted to share every night together in the same bed. Kexen couldn't imagine ever being without Ben at his side.

Kexen chose to wear another dress for the quickness of it, and when Ben slipped it over his head, he took the opportunity to say the words Kexen would never tire of hearing. "I love you, wife."

Kexen looked at his husband with adoration. "How did we get to be so lucky?"

"I suppose we owe it all to honey, mead and iron."

"Such simple things to bring such joy. Do you think you'll be able to convince Prince Soren to advocate for a trading treaty with Far Isle?"

"I will do my best. The people of Far Isle don't deserve to suffer for the perfidy of someone who cared nothing for them. I'm convinced that Magnus operated on his own agenda and not that of his nation. We'll have plenty of cheap iron ore from Amira, and it's worth the goodwill to pass it along to those in need."

Kexen gnawed at this lower lip, the topic bringing to the surface something that he couldn't put aside. "Maybe the king will send you on a special diplomatic mission there."

Ben shook his head. "No, I promised you that all of that is in the past." He started to leave the room.

Kexen stopped him with a hand to Ben's chest. "I wouldn't mind…really. It could be fun. I rather liked being a diplomat's wife—except for the part where we were imprisoned and you were tortured and we had to fight for our lives."

Ben put his finger to Kexen's lips. "We shall see." He held out his hand. "For now, Lady Tentrees, we must greet our visitors."

Kexen put his own hand into the safety of his husband's, and they went out to greet their guests as the noble and loving couple that they were.

Want to see more from this author?
Here's a taster for you to enjoy!

Treaty Brides: Stolen Bride
Samantha Cayto

Coming August 2022

Excerpt

"Drink up, your highness. You're falling behind."

Ronan, younger son of the king of Moorcondia, shot his companion the kind of prideful grin that he'd carefully cultivated since arriving at the university. "Alas, I have to leave for an assignation with a lady and can't afford to be too much in my cups." He slid the glass of beer back in the direction of his classmate.

The boy barked out a laugh and clapped Ronan on his shoulder with the kind of bone-jarring exuberance that seemed so common among boys of their age. Ronan didn't understand why every interaction had to turn into a contest of inflicting pain and humiliation. The others thought it all hilarious, reinforcing what he'd known for most of his life. He was not like them, not like any boy he'd ever met.

Not even his studious older brother thought anything strange about the rough and tumble lives of their male friends. It was merely that as the future ruler of their country, Morlen had the weight of duty on his shoulders and had to prepare for the time he would ascend to the throne. Such was the fate of the one of them who'd come out of the womb first, even by mere moments. He joined them when he could for nights of drinking and carousing, careful always not to do anything to tarnish his reputation. As the 'spare' in the family, Ronan had no expectations and could do most anything he liked. *No, not really.* He was only able to get away with what people thought a young, rich man would do. Too bad those were things he didn't like at all.

He didn't let his desires show on his face and instead bade his companions a good night. They gave him a raucous send-off, filled with innuendos of what they assumed he would get up to and demanding a full report the next day. He joined in the merriment with rehearsed bravado. "Now, lads, you know a gentleman never speaks of what happens between the sheets. I shall only say that I'm glad we don't have classes tomorrow."

Ronan threw on his heavy cloak and braced for the chilly night he knew waited for him outside. Spring was only grudgingly arriving, but his semester of classes would soon come to an end, and he could return to Moorcondia for the summer recess. It would be a relief to finally go home. This first year of university had proven more taxing than he'd expected. It wasn't his studies. It was the strain of keeping up his pretense of being a profligate rake. No one forced him to play this charade. Morlen certainly didn't care. But Ronan feared that if he didn't present the image of masculinity that everyone expected, they would easily see inside him, to his true self. He wasn't sure he could bear the scorn he felt certain would come his way.

I am a coward.

He considered, as he had many times, asking his parents to let him drop out. A university education was relatively new among the royal family. They might not care if he came back or not. But if he didn't, what would he do then? No matter how everyone had become accustomed to his uncle's new wife, Ronan wasn't so stupid as to assume his family and the members of court would accept him in any role other than an advisor to his brother. He would be expected to marry the proper noblewoman to add to the next generation of the family. That was his destiny, and staying at university helped put that eventuality off for a few years. There was value in that.

Ronan's personal guard, a somewhat grizzled man who was nonetheless capable of breaking a man's neck with a single twist, pushed away from the wall he'd been holding up in the drinking house and silently followed in Ronan's wake. He hated having to be chained to someone else all the time, but one older man who held no interest for him and kept his opinions to himself wasn't so bad, although the man's silent censure was often palpable. It was better than the contingent of younger guards who surrounded Morlen day and night—not that anyone really thought they were at risk here in this seat of learning… Still, it was important for the realm as well as each of them personally that they be safe from any violence. With Sir Frauk at his back, no one dared so much as shoot an angry look at him. Ronan simply had to pretend he didn't care about being shadowed by another who undoubtedly gave the king regular reports on how his younger son was running wild. His whole life had become one long effort at play-acting. It felt as if no one truly understood who and what he was, not even his twin.

Ronan tugged his cloak closer as he walked through the nearly empty streets of the old city, the sound of Sir Frauk's heavy-booted tread behind him. Monks had settled here long ago, attracting more people and founding a community. Starting a place of higher learning had come naturally to those original men, and now the university was surrounded by a vibrant city that existed on the edge of Moorcondia. It was a hub of trading, as well, attracting commerce from all over, except from those people who dwelled in the Dark Mountains. They kept to themselves, enigmas as much as the land where they lived. The craggy rocks were not inviting and rose high into the clouds.

They cast a looming shadow over this part of the city in particular — not surprising, given that this was where one went for less savory pursuits. The boys at the university considered it a badge of courage that they ventured here late at night. Ronan despised it and couldn't wait to reach his apartments. All he wanted to do was take a relaxing bath and curl up in bed with a good book. He could picture his valet waiting patiently for his return. Unlike Frauk, Igon was quick to show his disapproval of Ronan's nighttime pursuits. But once he'd settled Ronan into bed, he left him blessedly alone.

Ronan picked up his pace with eyes on the uneven cobblestones to ensure that he didn't slip. The fashionable boots he wore pleased him, but they weren't very sturdy. The last thing he wanted was for Frauk to think it was drink that made him stumble. The man suddenly uttered a muted cry, very unlike him. Ronan turned to see why and froze at the sight of the large soldier crashing to the ground. Another man, little more than a dark figure, heavily armed, loomed over him. Ronan stepped forward, although to do what he couldn't fathom. He was terrible at the martial arts and didn't possess so much as knife on him.

A rush of air and a flicker of something out of the corner of his eye was all the warning he got before someone grabbed him from behind. He was swept off his feet, and a cloth was pressed against his nose and mouth. Trained in warfare as he was, he instinctively started to put up a fight. Whoever had him, though, was far stronger, the man's massive arm holding him around his chest in a vise-like grip. And there was something soaking the gag, a sweet smell that made his head swim. As he fought to regain his freedom, the drug caused his muscles to go lax. Then there was nothing.

* * * *

Ronan came to with a pounding headache and a thick tongue. It took him a moment or two to assess his situation. It was night still, only now he was among the trees of a dense forest, not the stone buildings of the city. And he was on horseback, the gentle swaying of such a beast well-known to him. But he wasn't riding so much as being carried astride. His head and back were propped against a hard, yet warm, wall. He might have drifted back to sleep due to the rather pleasant location, except the circumstances of his attack came to him in a flash. Popping open his eyes farther, he struggled to gain freedom.

An arm that had lain loosely against his waist tightened. "Easy, your highness. I have you securely on my mount."

Those were not comforting words, given the situation, and they were uttered with an accent that was unfamiliar to him. They rumbled through the broad chest against which he was being held. He tried to claw that arm away, but covered as it was in thick leather bands, he had no impact. It was while he did so that he noticed there were others riding around them, slipping in and out of his field of vision among the trees. To a man they were large, imposing figures dressed in dark clothing. They reminded him of the evil specters he'd seen illustrated in one of his favorite books. He wasn't so fanciful, however, as to believe them to be anything other than men who wished him harm, so he opened his mouth to yell for help.

His captor's hand clapped across his lips before he could utter a sound. "We have not yet cleared the outer farms of the city. If you scream, men may come running to your rescue, and we'll be forced to kill them. I don't want that. Do you?"

There was something about the man's tone that skittered up Ronan's spine and made him shudder. It wasn't fear, although that was there in abundance. It was a different kind of emotional reaction that nevertheless frightened him, too. He shook his head, because the man seemed to be waiting for a reply, and of course, the last thing Ronan wanted was for his father's subjects to die in vain on his behalf.

"Good. Now do I have your word that if I remove my hand, you won't cry out?"

Galling as it was, Ronan nodded, and when his mouth was liberated, he kept his promise. That didn't mean he would stay silent. He tried to turn to look at his captor. "What do you think you are doing?"

The man stared down at him, his broad, close-bearded face partially concealed by the nose plate of his helmet. "Kidnapping you."

Ronan huffed in indignation. "I am aware of *that*. Why? What do you want from me?"

"From you, nothing much."

"You must be seeking money. I have access to plenty of coin if you take me back to the city." Surely that was all it would take for this nightmare to end.

"I don't want your money." The infuriating man spoke as if they discussed the weather and not Ronan's fate, whatever that might be.

Reaching inside his shirt, Ronan pulled out the simple, yet very valuable, dark sapphire pendant his mother had given him on his eighteenth birthday. Morlen had received one exactly like it, masculine and beautiful at the same time. "If not that, what about this? Take it and leave me to find my way back." He knew there was a flaw to his logic. The man could yank the necklace from Ronan's neck and still hold him for ransom. Perhaps the guy and his cohorts weren't very bright.

The man huffed what might have been a laugh. "Your trinket doesn't interest me in the least."

That answer stunned Ronan into silence. The pendant was very valuable, he was sure. His mother would never give her sons anything less. Nothing about this misadventure made any sense. And as they traveled deeper into unknown territory, Ronan had to work to suppress his growing fear.

"Then tell me what you want!" He was careful to keep his voice down but couldn't hide his emotions, never could.

"It is complicated. Here and now is not the time or place to explain. We'll make camp for a short while once we have crossed the Moorcondian border. For now, you need do nothing more than rest, if that is your wont. As I said, I have you securely on my steed." There was silence for the space of a few horse steps, then, "I won't let anything bad happen to you."

As ridiculous as that reassurance was, it nevertheless sent something like relief coursing through Ronan. Encircled in the man's powerful arms, he perversely did feel safe, if one didn't count the danger the man himself presented. "You mean other than being knocked unconscious by some drug and stolen away by brigands for the gods know what reason?"

There was a pause. "Yes, other than that. And I don't know about your gods, but the All Mother understands what is at stake and sees what is in my heart. This is necessary."

"So you say." Ronan couldn't help fuming. Another thought popped into his aching head. "What of Sir Frauk? You killed *him*." While he'd resented the man's presence, he hated the idea that he'd died trying to save him.

"We did no such thing. He was knocked out, tied up and we even found a reasonably warm place for him to remain until he wakes."

"You're lying." Ronan knew brigands, especially those who ransomed wealthy people, had no scruples.

"Why would I bother to do so? You are already furious, yet well within my control. There would be no benefit to lying about the fate of your man."

Ronan had to admit to himself that there was some logic in what his captor said. He kept that observation to himself, however, and said no more. His head still ached, and he was exhausted. There was nothing he could do to free himself at the moment. The only option open to him was to bide his time and hope for a chance at escape. He tried to keep himself upright instead of leaning against his abductor, but his fatigue mixed with the gentle rhythm of the horse's movement made that impossible. As hard as the man's chest was, it made for a decent resting place. Ronan couldn't keep his eyes open.

"Who are you, anyway?" he managed to ask in a sleepy voice.

"I am Jarl Tarben of the Dark Mountains."

That information intrigued Ronan as much as it alarmed him. He'd never before met anyone from that mysterious and isolated country. But as the man had called him 'your highness' he undoubtedly knew the prize he possessed. With the last of his strength, Ronan used that identity as a warning. "I am Ronan, prince of Moorcondia. My father the king will have your head for this."

The man sighed silently, only the movement of his chest telling the tale. "Well, he can try."

Ronan made an effort to rally with a retort, but he was too tired to do so. Besides, even as he issued the threat, he wasn't sure he wanted that outcome.

* * * *

Tarben glanced down at the top of his captive's sleeping head. He knew that the foul stuff he'd used to knock the boy out was to blame, but also understood that it was easier to find solace in sleep than to face the fear of what was to become of him. While Tarben knew that he would keep the prince safe, there was no way for the boy to know that. It would take time to prove it through actions, although matters between them would get worse — far worse — before they got better. *If they ever do.*

The idea of being tied to someone who loathed him for the rest of his life was unpleasant, to say the least. Not that there was a choice. His duty to the people of the Dark Mountains took precedence over all other considerations, including his own happiness. He might not be his sire's heir, but he was still bound by the obligations of being the man's son. The distasteful act of kidnapping the Moorcondian prince was necessary, the last, best hope his people had. He would do this, as there was no choice. All he could hope was that he could make a decent life for the boy slumped against him.

It wouldn't be any kind of hardship for him. The slender form resting against his chest stirred strong feelings in him. There was the urge to protect someone smaller and weaker, that was true enough. His reaction was more than that, though. Prince Ronan was the type of man who had always appealed to Tarben. He liked someone lithe in his bed who fit easily against his shoulder. A small, tight rump was a particular weakness of his. Just the feel of it pressed against his groin was sufficient to make him hard, even with the layers of thick clothing between them. And thank the All Mother for that. The last thing he wanted was to add to the lad's fright by prodding him with a stiff cock. Tarben would never impose that part of himself on anyone. It was the single thing he could control in this whole miserable affair. When he'd made that silent vow to himself, he hadn't counted on being as attracted to the Moorcondian prince as he was. Living a chaste life wasn't an appealing vision of his future, but such was the price of privilege — for both of them. They were second sons and duty-bound to play their roles in unexpected ways.

The slow passage through the dark forest made it easy for him to get lost in his thoughts. It was a monotonous journey, although knowing he was nearly at the border with his own country bettered his mood. There was no one following them. Those of his men whose job it was to protect their back and wipe their trails as much as possible would cry out a warning if that changed. The rest of the soldiers ranged around them, a quiet escort that showed as familiar shadows in the gloom. He knew that he—and by extension Ronan—were as safe as they could be. These were Tarben's hand-picked men, those he trusted the most out of all his father's force of fighters. Once they crossed the narrow river that hugged the border, they would meet up with the others. His father and the cousin who advised him had insisted on a larger contingent, just in case the Moorcondians had more palace guards watching over the prince than was known.

Normally Tarben would be suspicious of the ease with which the prince had been snatched, but in this case, he was confident that no such back-up had existed. Apparently, King Auden was unconcerned for his second's son's safety, perhaps because it was obvious that this boy would never be a fighter and therefore not worthy of anyone else's attention. Or it might simply be that the man was as heartless about his own child as he was about the plight of his Dark Mountains neighbors.

The sound of rushing water reached his ears, sending a small amount of relief through him. Once they had crossed the river, they would be in friendly territory that he and his men knew like the backs of their hands. But they had not reached safety yet and needed to remain vigilant for trouble, even a naturally occurring one. Early spring thawing from the mountains fed the river, making it icy cold and treacherously fast. He wasn't overly worried, because they'd traveled from here a scant day ago and had crossed without mishap. Their warhorses were sturdy and sure-footed beasts. Nevertheless, he watched how well his vanguard maneuvered the crossing before moving forward to do the same. As he approached the slippery bank, he tightened his grip on his passenger, surprisingly concerned about making sure he didn't slip off. That effort in turn caused the boy to rouse.

"What's happening?"

Tarben hated the alarm in his captive's voice. "Easy, boy. We are crossing the river that boarders our two countries. Once on the other side, you will be in the Kingdom of the Dark Mountains." His reassurances fell on deaf ears. Ronan grabbed hold of Tarben's arm and tried to twist to look behind them. The sudden movement caused the horse to become skittish. Tarben easily brought it back under control before admonishing the prince more harshly than he'd intended.

"Be still! If you fall into the water, I will be forced to jump in after you, and I don't relish freezing my balls off. There is no one coming to your rescue, in any event," he added more kindly. "You are mine now." He hadn't intended to be so possessive, yet his own words caused something to well up deep inside him.

Prince Ronan didn't give him a chance to dwell on that, however. He squirmed in Tarben's hold a bit before settling down with a noticeable shudder. "What are you going to do to me?" There were tears showing in his voice.

Tarben had to harden his heart, even as he sought to soothe the boy. "I won't hurt you, but you and I are both insignificant parts of a serious game that can mean the difference between life and death for thousands. I told you I would explain matters later. We are nearly at the point at which we can rest for a while."

His captive didn't fight him anymore, simply sat with his back straight so as not to lean against Tarben's chest. He missed the contact, although he was hardly in a position to complain. He was not the aggrieved party in this drama. As soon as his horse's hooves clomped in the mud on the other side, his father's waiting warriors appeared at the tree line to greet them. The prince gasped and actually shrank against Tarben now. It would have been delightful if not born of fear.

"Those are my men. They intend you no harm."

"As if you and I have the same definition of what that means," the prince sneered.

That small show of defiance pleased Tarben. The Moorcondian appeared delicate, but he wasn't weak or cowed. Tarben sought a different way to reassure him. "I shall be the only man to touch you from this point forward."

"Is that supposed to bring me comfort?"

"It is all I have to give." It saddened Tarben that it was true.

He rode into the middle of the makeshift camp his men had formed and stopped his horse near the fire in the middle. One of the soldiers came to take hold of the horse's reins to make it easier for Tarben to dismount. He did so, keeping one hand on Ronan and the other on the saddle, then he pulled his captive off and set him on his feet. The boy didn't fight him, but his knees started to buckle as soon as Tarben tried to release him. Instead, he took a firmer grip, this time around his waist, and led him away from the horse and over to the fire. His men stared at the Moorcondian prince with open curiosity and, for some, hostility. Tarben used his own glare to remind them they were to show his captive the respect his station deserved.

"Here, you will bed down by the fire for warmth."

The prince dug in his heels. "I need to relieve myself."

"Of course." Tarben did as well, now that it had been mentioned. "I'll take you to a place of privacy."

There was little to be had of that in a soldiers' encampment, and no one cared about exposing themselves in such situations anyway. Ronan was different—in Tarben's view at least. The boy deserved to be sheltered from prying eyes—all those except Tarben's, that was. He led Ronan to a spot behind a big tree and let him go as soon as he was sure the boy could stand on his own. Sweeping aside the apron of his leather breastplate, he plucked at the laces of his breeches while keeping an eye on his captive.

Ronan grimaced. "Must you stand so close?"

"Alas, I must. I can tell you are weighing the idea of bolting for freedom. I need to be able to stop that nonsense before it happens."

The boy shot him a look of pure hatred. "You think me silly for trying to regain my freedom?"

"I do when it means running through an unknown forest with many dangers lurking. Even if you don't risk drowning by trying to cross the river, there are wild beasts, including men, who would bring an end to you before you even knew that you were under attack. I must keep you safe from that."

The prince looked away on a huff and eventually managed to relieve himself, even with Tarben so close. Tarben had no difficulty, naturally, and waited patiently, giving as much privacy as he could until the boy was done. He led him back to the camp, not quite holding on to him, but with his hand hovering near, just in case it became necessary. Desperate people, like animals, couldn't be trusted to act rationally. Once they reached the fire, Tarben waved at the fur pallet laid down for their comfort. "Here's where we spend the rest of the night. I'll have water and some food brought first."

Instead of sitting, the prince crossed his arms and glared at him mulishly. "You said you'd tell me what this is all about. I want to know now what you are going to do with me."

Understanding that the time had come to explain their unusual fate, Tarben steeled himself for the virulent, possibly violent, reaction he was going to get. He looked the boy straight in the eyes as he answered. "I'm going to marry you."

About the Author

Samantha Cayto is a Boston-area native who practices as a business lawyer by day while writing erotic romance at night—the steamier the better. She likes to push the envelope when it comes to writing about passion and is delighted other women agree that guy-on-guy sex is the hottest ever.

She lives a typical suburban life with her husband, three kids and four dogs. Her children don't understand why they can't read what she writes, but her husband is always willing to lend her a hand—and anything else—when she needs to choreograph a scene.

Samantha loves to hear from readers. You can find her contact information, website details and author profile page at https://www.pride-publishing.com

PUBLISHING

Sign up for our newsletter and find out about all our romance book releases, eBook sales and promotions, sneak peeks and FREE romance books!